THE
DRUMMER
OF THE
ELEVENTH
NORTH
DEVONSHIRE
FUSILIERS

by GUY DAVENPORT

North Point Press
San Francisco   1990

ACKNOWLEDGMENTS

"A Gingham Dress" is reprinted with the kind permission of the *Santa Monica Review*, "Badger" with the
kind permission of *Conjunctions*. A shorter version of
"Colin Maillard" was published in *Granta*. My few
readers will recognize that "*Wo es war, soll ich wer-
den*" completes a trilogy begun with *Apples and Pears*
(North Point Press, 1984) and *The Jules Verne Steam
Balloon* (North Point Press, 1987). Freud's phrase, in
which Jacques Lacan heard pre-Socratic eloquence,
comes from his *Neue Vorlesungen* (lecture 31) and is a
bone of contention among interpreters and transla-
tors. "Colin Maillard" exfoliates from a photograph
by Bernard Faucon; "Juno of the Veii" derives from
Plutarch's *Life of Camillus*. Tom White's execution is
history; all the rest I have imagined.

LIBRARY OF CONGRESS
CATALOGING-IN-PUBLICATION DATA
Davenport, Guy.
  The drummer of the Eleventh North Devonshire
  Fusiliers / by Guy Davenport.
    p.   cm.
  ISBN 0-86547-447-8
  I. Title.
  PS3554.A86D78   1990
  813'.54—dc20   90-36968

CONTENTS

The Drummer of the

Eleventh North

Devonshire Fusiliers

Colin Maillard

Down the slope of the knoll by the river six boys herded a seventh. Their school, partly brick turrets, partly modern slabs of rectilinear glass, was far behind them, inserted into a line of cedars across the horizon. There were puffs of white clouds in the bright blue sky. Down on the river a farmer was burning off a field. Further up the slope a woman in long skirts was collecting butterflies in a net. Her straw gardening hat was kept in place by a red scarf tied under her chin.

Every attempt of the seventh, smaller boy to break and run for it was thwarted by blocking shoulders and quick footwork.

Up from the meadow where six Holsteins grazed stood a post that had once held a salt lick, or been part of a gate, or of some structure the rest of which had long since been carried away. Wind and rain had made it smooth and gray.

Aage, Bo, Martin, and Peder wore white kneepants and blue sweatshirts. Ib was in American jeans, and Bent wore short pants, like the little boy Tristan.

—Stand, Aage said to Tristan, still and easy. I'll do the rest.

—Martin and Peder, Bo said, are going to fight.

—Not till after, Martin said.

—And not here, Peder said. Back of the hill, and in our underpants, so's not to get blood on our clothes.

—Crazy, Ib said.

Tristan stood, worried and submissive, while Aage unbuttoned his blouse and took it off with a flourish.

—Hang it on the post, he instructed Martin.

Aage worked Tristan's undershirt up. His voice was calm and menacing. A few more unfastenings and pulls, and Tristan stood mother-naked, cheeks and ears the color of a radish.

—Here in the sack, Peder said.

He shook out a dress, blue with white dots, a frilled hem, and a pink ribbon through the lace at the collar.

—Sexy, Bent said.

—Looks more like a nightgown, said Bo.

— You're going to make me wear a dress? Tristan asked.

—We told you not to talk, Aage said. Stick your arms through the sleeves.

—It's only a game, Martin said. Isn't it, Ib? Ib doesn't tell lies.

—Not only a game, Ib said, but a game with the rules backward. You're It, we decided last night, and instead of you having the blindfold, we are the blindfoldeds.

—Except for the haircut, he looks like a girl.

—What for? Tristan asked.

—The more you talk, Aage said, the worse it's going to be for you, squirt.

—Pigeon to the Master, Bo said, and you'll wish you were dead.

—This is the drill, Bent said. We're blindfolded, you're not. If you were to get clean away, slim chance, you can't go back, not in a dress.

—What happens when you catch me?

—We told you not to talk.

Aage looked at Bo, merry with a secret, and Bo flipped his fingers against his blue sweatshirt. Bent zipped down the fly of his short pants and crossed his eyes. Ib guffawed. Martin glared at Peder, Peder at Martin.

A skipper on flixweed opened its wings twice before darting off, with a dip, zigzag and fluttery.

—*Sylvestris Poda*, Tristan said. I don't care. Give me the sniffles, this dress.

Aage bound Bo's eyes with a scout kerchief, Bent Ib, and on around until they were all blindfolded, except Tristan, who stood miserable and confused in his dress. Bo's white quiff stuck up like a grebe's tail from the scarf belting his eyes, and they all moved like windup toys.

In every direction there were green and brown fields, and a silver sliver of sea to the west.

—You're there, somewhere, Aage said. If you talk, or holler, we'll know where you are, and get you.

They began to mill, with stiff arms and open hands.

—It's me, you've got, smugger, Bo said. Feel for a dress.

—There was an owl, a Great Gray, *Strix nebulosa*, on a limb, Bent said, on the fir.

Tristan ducked Ib's flailing grope.

—Outside my window.

—We could all be frigging each other, Peder said, in brotherly bliss.

Nipped under Aage's reach, changing course like a rabbit.

—Not Peder and Martin: they're going to fight.

—Same thing, Bo said.

It was not bright to think of green graph paper and algebra when who knew what was about to happen to him, but Tristan did.

—Everybody stand still. Blind people can feel what's around them.

Or of the yellow willow by the river and the heron that stood on one leg downstream from it.

—Wind.

—Arms out.

—Turn slow, all of us in close.

—We could hold hands, in a circle, and move in.

—If he's inside.

—He's inside. Aren't you, Tristan?

Silence.

He could see. They couldn't. No reason why they should ever catch him.

—The owl was looking in at our window.

—Which blinded him.

Thing was, to make no noise and to account for every direction at once. Stay on your toes, stay down, keep turning.

—Who groped my crotch? Martin asked.

—Peder, probably, Bo said.

Bent, squirming away from Ib, made a wide opening in the circle, through which Tristan nipped, and walked backward, on his toes. Then he turned and ran as fast as he could. From the dip on the other side of the knoll he could see the woman with her butterfly net, the farmer burning off his field. The shine had gone off the sea. He minded being barefoot more than the dress. The dress was like a dream, and no fault of his, but to have let his shoes be taken away from him was lack of character.

—Bullies, he said out loud. And unfair.

But he'd fooled them, there was that. And he would never know what they would have done to him if they'd caught him.

—Don't think like that! he said, stomping his foot.

If he made a big circle, he could get back to the school without being caught, provided it was a good while before they realized he'd given them the slip.

If he were in Iceland, or on Fyn, there would be ponies he could commandeer and ride. If he were on the other side of the school, there would be a road, with cars. It would be grand if a helicopter choppered down, with police or soldiers, to rescue him, deliver him in glory to the school, having kindly given him a flight jacket to wear over this miserable dress. And the woman netting butterflies was too far inside the long way around he had to circle. If his luck held, he could be a long way ahead of them before the pack was on his heels.

He kept to the sides of knolls. His breathing was wet and sharp, as when you're taking a cold.

Heather and bracken and gorse and knotgrass, and all as fast in rubble as a cat's tail in a cat. All people with socks and sneakers were rich, didn't they know? And pants. And did his balls feel good because he was free? If he was: they might be tearing after him, with longer legs, and with shoes, and here he was crying, like a baby.

Where you are is how you feel. Back there, dipping under their trawling arms, pivoting on his heel, ducking and dashing, there was no time: everything happened at once. And then time turned on again.

He didn't dare look back. For one thing, every direction now looked the same. For another, he didn't want to know if they were behind him in a pack, or worse, fanning out, to come at him on all sides.

A stitch in your ribs goes away, he knew, if you keep running, and there was second wind, good old second wind. And luck, there was luck.

Had the sky ever been emptier or everywhere so far away?

Luck, he felt in his bones, had a warrant for his safe passage over these scrub meadows. The wood's edge would be just beyond the next rise, or the next. Then he could go along the wood, even disappear into it, if need be. There was a longish stretch of open fields after that, before the next wood, but that one had paths in it, and through it he could get back to the school.

But he had to go around hills, not over them, where they could see him.

What was all this about, anyway? Playing Colin Maillard with the rules reversed, and him in a dress? Aage he'd suspect anything of, always ready for a jape as he was, especially if it was a way of sucking up to Bo. Bent was a mean little rat to be in on this. How did Ib get mixed up in it?

His nose stung inside, and the back of his mouth.

He'd cut the underside of two toes, the little one on his left foot, the long one beside the big toe on his right. His knees hurt. His shins hurt.

He stumbled and fell sprawling.

I will not cry, he heard himself saying. I will fucking not fucking cry.

When he got up, he couldn't believe that the use of his left ankle was not his anymore. The pain would go away. Luck wouldn't do something like this to him. It absolutely wouldn't. He needed all the luck he could get.

Worse, he heard voices.

The voices made him angry. It was wonderfully easy now not to blubber, not to even think of defeat. He was going to get away. A whonky ankle wasn't going to stop him.

The voices were to his left. They weren't a hue and cry. They were mingled in with each other. Ib's he recognized, and Aage's. He heard *all this crap about a fair fight* and *we won't stop you.*

He forgot that his ankle wouldn't work, and fell again. Where *were* they?

On the other side of the knoll to his left. He remembered: Martin and Peder were to fight. He hated fights. They were more senseless, even, than making him wear a dress to play *blindebuk* backward.

The whole stupid world was crazy. Plus it didn't seem to notice.

He gave up hopping, and crawled toward the top of the knoll. There was a big rock he could lie flat behind, and look. Their minds, at least, weren't on him anymore. There was sweet relief in that. And they wouldn't pick on him when he had a hurt ankle.

Aage and Bo were with Martin, who was stripped down to his undershorts. Peder was undressing, throwing his clothes to Ib and Bent. He had smaller undershorts than Martin, blue with a white waistband. They'd left on their socks and sneakers, as the ground in the hollow where they were was as rocky and scrubby as the fields he'd run so fast over.

The late afternoon was filling the hollow with shadow. Aage was whispering in Martin's ear. Bo sat, Martin's clothes in his lap.

Peder walked over and stood nose to nose with Martin, talking very low between clenched teeth. His hands tightened into fists. Martin was breathing fast, his chest jumping as if he'd run farther and harder than Tristan.

But they hadn't run at all. He saw that he'd apparently been making a steady turn to the left, when all the while he thought he was running in a straight line. The post where they'd played Colin Maillard was the next knoll over. Talk about unlucky.

He was scared. He hated what he was seeing, and didn't want to see. Martin and Peder almost touching, breathing into each other's mouths, looking into each other's eyes as if trying to look into each other's heads. Aage stood eerily still, waiting, with a strange expression on his face. Bo's knees were quivering. Ib had his hands on his hips, legs wide apart. Bent was licking his lips.

Peder hit first, a jab into Martin's midriff that sounded like a melon splitting and doubled Martin over. Before he could straighten up, Peder kicked him in the chest, a fierce football punt of a kick that made him fall backward.

Tristan closed his eyes and pushed his face against the ground. He heard grunts, ugly words, scuffling.

Aage, Bo, Ib, and Bent were saying nothing at all.

When he dared a look, Peder was on top of Martin, pummeling his face with both fists, which were bloody. Martin's legs were flailing against the ground.

Tristan was halfway down the slope, running with a dipping limp, before he realized that he had moved at all.

—Make him quit! he was shouting.

Bo looked up at him in surprise. Aage grinned.

—Keep back, he said. A fight's a fight.

With a porpoise heave and flop, Martin twisted from under Peder, jabbed his knee into his crotch, and pulled free. Peder's face was white with pain, his mouth making the shape of a scream. Martin was bleeding from the nose in spurts, and he was sobbing in convulsions, his shoulders jolting. He wiped the blood from his mouth, and fell on Peder with both fists hammering on his terrified face.

Tristan locked his arms around Martin's waist and pulled.

—Help me get him off, you assholes! he shouted. You fucking stupid shits!

—Stay out of this, Aage shouted. It's none of your fucking business.

—Where'd he come from, anyway? Ib asked.

By tightening his armlock and pushing as hard as he could, Tristan rolled Martin off Peder, who got up with a paralytic jerk, gagging. Backing away on knees and elbows, he retched and puked.

Bo said quietly:

—I think they've fought enough.

—Me too, Bent said.

—Oh shit, Aage said. They haven't even begun. Shove Tristan baby there toward the school with a foot against his ass, so's we'll have boys only again, and let's get on with it.

—I think they've fought enough, Aage, Bo repeated. Something's wrong with Martin. There's too much blood.

—How can we get them to the infirmary, Bent asked with a scared voice, without all of us getting it in the neck?

—Cripes! Ib said. Peder's conked out.

—Fainted.

—Knocked out.

—Shake him.

—Get the puke out of his mouth.

—Let the bastard die, Martin said, spitting blood. Turn me loose, Tristan.

Bo and Ib lifted Peder by the shoulders, trying to get him to sit up.

—Don't like the way his head lolls, Bo said.

—He's coming around. Look at his eyes.

—They'll never get cleaned up and get back to school looking as if they haven't had a fight. It's a fucking war, here.

—Who says the fight's over? Aage asked.

—Oh shut up, you stinking sadist, Tristan said. You're mental, you know that?

Aage, pretending speechlessness, covered his mouth with both hands.

—Peder! Bo hollered. Are you all right?

—Look, Ib said, we've got Peder unconscious and maybe bleeding to death, huh, and we're acting like morons. Let's do something.

—Do what?

—Carry him to the infirmary, for starters.

—Let him die, Martin said.

—Wipe some of the blood off with Tristan's dress, Bo said. Take it off. Go get your clothes, on the post next hill over.

—Can't, Tristan said. Turned my ankle running from you pigs, and can't go that far.

—I'll get them, Bent said.

—So off with the dress. Let's rip it in two, half for Martin, half for Peder.

—Peder's opening his eyes.

—The whole point of the fight, Aage said, was for somebody to win it. You can't have a fight without a winner and a loser.

—Stuff it, Ib said.

—And fuck it, Martin said. I've had it. If Peder has too. He, by God, looks it.

—No way, Ib said, we can keep this from Master. Looks like a train hit both of you.

Tristan stood naked as an eft, on one leg. Ib kept spitting on the wad he'd made of the halved dress, wiping blood off Martin.

Peder waved Bo away, who was trying to do the same for him.

—Stand him up, Bent said. See if he can.

Peder gave him the finger, scrambled up, and pitched forward, to vomit again.

—What, Tristan asked, was the fight about, anyway?

—You don't want to know, Ib said. Can you walk on that leg?

—Sure, Tristan said, I think so.

—All we need right now, Bent said, is for somebody to come along to see two of us looking like a slaughterhouse and one naked cripple. Master would eat pills for the next two days.

—Turn anybody's stomach, Tristan said. Turns mine. Fighting's stupid, you know?

—If anybody asked your opinion, Aage said.

—Why did you make me play blindman's bluff in a dress? Look, I'm not afraid of any of you, huh? And I'm not taking any more bullying, OK?

—Would you fucking listen? Aage said.

Bo mopped Martin. Ib and Bent helped Peder up, whose knees were trembling.

—I'm all right, Peder said, his voice thick. Just let me alone a bit.

He pulled off his briefs to wipe his face. He felt his testicles with cautious fingers.

—Still there.

—Bo, Peder said, feel my balls and see if you think anything's wrong. One word out of anybody, and you get it in the mouth, I fucking promise.

—The rules were no rules, Aage said, so you can't bitch about kneed balls.

—Since when were you God? Tristan asked.

—Nobody's whining, Aage, Peder said. You get a knee in your balls and see if you don't puke.

—Let Martin feel, Bo said. He did it, and that's where it started, and you've got to make up. That's what a fight's for, yes?

—Up on the hill, Bent said, when I fetched Tristan's clothes, which you might put on after I went to the trouble, good deed and all, you know, the woman murdering butterflies seemed to be drifting this way. She's the one who glares at us on the way to the candy store.

—How did whichwhat start with Peder's balls? Tristan asked. All my togs are inside out.

—Do we let Tristan in? Bo asked. We've made him bust his ankle, and he did give us the slip.

—Ib and Bo and me, we vote yes, Bent said. Martin? Peder?

—He's too little, Martin said. Or is he?

—Feel my balls, Martin, Peder said. See if they're OK. I'm not mad anymore.

—Let me, Aage said. I'll give you a straight answer.

—No, Peder said. Martin. And there's a damned tooth loose.

—It was you that wanted to fight, Martin said.

—So let's have your opinion as to whether I'm ever going to be a father.

—What's *in*? Tristan asked. I have two toes about to come off, if anybody's interested, to go with my bum ankle.

—There's a poor imitation of a creek on the far side of the wood, you know, Ib said. We can get the blood off Martin and Peder.

—But not the bruises, fat lips, and shiners.

—My balls are going to look like a black grapefruit. What do you think, Martin?

—If you come OK, next time you jack off, then they aren't busted, right? Let's see the tooth.

—What am I in? Tristan asked.

—What's your vote, Aage?

Aage shrugged and quiddled his fingers.

—I'm already outvoted. I steal the dress, I solve Peder and Martin's problem, I invent inside-out Colin Maillard, and all at once I'm a clown.

—Life's like that, Peder said.

—Look, Bo said, it's getting cold out here. Let's head out, the shortest way back, and to every question we answer absofuckinglutely nothing. Stare right over the top of the head of anybody asking any question. OK?

All nodded, including Tristan.

They cast long, rippling shadows on the brown meadows, Bo carrying Tristan piggyback, Aage with his hands in his pockets, Martin and Peder each with an arm around the other's shoulders, Ib and Bent skipping along behind.

Juno of the Veii

Terra-cotta she was, and her hands were on her breasts, offering milk. Her big kindly eyes were painted white, with blue pupils. Long braided hair gilded, robe polychrome, Tuscan yellow stripes alternating with Sicilian green, silver sandals on her feet. Her expression was the way your mother looked at you in fun, playing that trick of love to cajole you into doing something you'd rather not.

She was the Juno of the Veii, and she was to be taken from her countrified temple to Rome.

Camillus had asked for pure youths to carry her on a litter, and the adjutant without a blink about-faced, looking wildly for a warrant officer. You rise in the ranks by obeying Camillus while the command is in the air between his beard and your ears.

—Clean, the adjutant said, scrubbed.

—Young, the sergeant said, means that they won't have had time to sin with any volume. Say recruits who aren't up to their eyes in debt, fresh of face, preferably with their milk teeth, calf's eyes, good stock, and washen hair.

—Take them to the flamen, the adjutant said, who'll get them into white tunics and clarify their minds for going into the *fanum* to bring the figure out, proper.

The first charge had been at dawn, and horrible. No trumpets.

—Use their roosters, the corporal said.

No guidons, no battle lines. Go in like creeping rats.

—Six *gregarii*, the sergeant said. We'll choose the best four. Wash them within an inch of their lives, dress their hair as if for a wedding.

We were all in a muck sweat from the siege. Some of us had burrowed under the wall, many of us were bloody, several had broken arms. The Falsicans had put up a fight, but with Camillus that has never got anybody anywhere.

The surrender was before noon.

—You are now Romans, Camillus said. Your enemies are our enemies.

There was fear in every face, and confusion. We tried to cheer them up with a parade around the walls.

Sistrum sistrum tympany horn.

And then Camillus had gone into their temple, being very religious, very correct. Meanwhile, we had the local wives filling tubs of water in the square. The sergeant kept lining up handsome privates with the straightest noses he could find, the broadest shoulders, trimmest waists, most soldierly legs. The priest was at them asking if they were virgins, if they were pious, what household gods they were devoted to, if they were distinguished enough to have participated in the cleansing of the trumpets on the Field of Mars, if they'd ever hunted without propitiating Diana afterward, if there was any incest, blasphemy, or habitual bad luck among them, and so on.

Though none admitted to virginity, the priest was not born yesterday, and came up with six tall striplings who washed in the tubs in the street, surrounded by a ring of staring children, pigs, and dogs. There were comments from the locals, which we understood by tone of voice alone. The priest went from tub to tub, casting spells on the water. The quartermaster brought a jug of oil and a jar of talcum.

—Do goats count?

—You mean sisters, don't you?

—What about with the sergeant?

—Boys, boys, the priest said. You are going to bear a *sacrum*. Suppress these scandalous, worldly *ioca*, out of reverence for Juno. Behind your ears, between your toes, under your foreskins. Scrub on those rusty knees.

We could see that the sergeant wanted to say *they have been in a battle, Your Grace*, but was restraining himself with his hands behind his back, keeping his dignity.

They dried with towels, oiled themselves, with jests saltier than in the tubs, strigiled down while being blessed by the priest, and repeated, with one degree of accuracy or another, a strange old prayer.

Camillus himself held inspection.

—Name, soldier?

—Lucius, sir.

—Are there impurities of mind or deed which would render you unclean for transporting the Mater of the Veii?

—No, sir.

—You realize the seriousness of your duty?

—Yes, sir.

—Name, soldier?

—Marcus, sir.

Same question, same answer, down the line. Burrus, the red down on whose cheeks made him look like a fox, and Caius, with rusty knees, were nominated supernumeraries.

Two rows of drummers lined the path to the temple, keeping back profane noises and such spirits of the air and the dead as might botch our enterprise.

Camillus, his way strewn with barley, went into the temple first.

No thunder sounded, only the tumbling warning of the drums.

The detail came behind him, looking more like altar boys than soldiers.

We heard later that he spoke in the old Latin, identifying himself as a child by adoption and favor of Mater Matuta, guardian of farmers and soldiers at dawn.

—I come worshipfully to beg your permission to take you to Rome, where you will have a house of honor among our great gods. I have clean young men of pure morals to carry you on their shoulders.

It was Marcus who was surest what then happened.

Roman generals do not bend for god or man. So Camillus stood at attention until she gave her sign.

Some of the detail said that the statue nodded, and spoke in darkest Etruscan, full of whistles and clicks, and this is what Camillus reported to the conscript fathers.

But Marcus said that she smiled.

A Gingham Dress

These butter peas are a dime the quart. Fifteen for the runners and a nickel the okra. Lattimer here picked the dewberries. He's a caution, ain't he? Going on nine and still won't wear nothing but a dress and bonnet. Says he's a girl, don't you, Lattimer? He's as cute as one. Everybody says that.

Say what, Leon? That's what I was telling Mrs. Fant. He'll grow out of it.

We'll be sure to bring watermelons when they're in. It's been so dry. Good for the corn but keeps the melons back. Our cantaloupes, I always say, are sweet as sugar. We stand good to have some next time down. The mushmelon, the honeydew, and the ice-box: we raise all three.

What, Lattimer? Of course Mrs. Fant has a ice-box. He likes to know what things people have in their houses. He was saying on the way down that he wished he could see ever bird in ever cage all over town.

We heard tell it was in the paper about the church up to Sandy Springs. Leon says it puts us on the map. Nothing to do with us. We go Baptist. These are the Pentecostals, church right at the turn off to Toccoa. The way I understand it is that their preacher went on vacation, to Florida, and he ast this Rev. Holroyd, from Seneca, to take his flock while he was away, you see. Well, first thing he saw was neckties on the men. And he said the Holy Bible is against any necktie. You ever hear such a thing? But they taken them off.

What, Leon? Leon says he thinks he'll join their church.

Our preacher, speaking of wearing and not wearing, don't know no better but what Lattimer is a girl. He comes to us on the Sunday only, from over to Piney Grove. Of course, you are, dear heart, if you say you are. On the Wednesday we get a lady preacher. Comes over from Saluda, regular as clockwork, and does a beautiful service. Sings, plays the piano, reads from Scripture just like a man. She knows that Lattimer is a boy. Knew it right off. She said first time she set eyes on him, *That's a boy in a dress.*

Leon says *Anybody would.* But this Mrs. Dillingham, Rev. Dillingham I ought to say, says she don't see why not. She says as long as he's not lewd, she sees no harm.

Anyway, here's Rev. Hunnicutt back from Florida and the first thing they ast him is do Christians wear neckties. What they wrote in the paper was that about half the church wanted Rev. Holroyd to stay on, as knowing Scripture better than Rev. Hunnicutt, and the other half was content with Hunnicutt, who says there's not a word in the Bible about any necktie.

It is funny, ain't it, Lattimer? He listens to every word you say, and remembers it. And sings along with the radio. He has a lovely voice, if I do say so. The Gospel Hour's his favorite. Holds his doll up and makes like it's singing, too. He helps in the kitchen, you know, as kindly as a daughter, and can wring a chicken's neck good as I can. Wants his hair long, but Leon draws the line there. So he's a girl with boy's hair.

You'll not regret them butter peas. They cook up best with salt pork, I always say. Let's see now, would you want some of Lattimer's dewberries, a pint?

This Roosevelt is something else, ain't he? They say he's a Jew. And his wife sits down and eats with niggers. I never seen the beat.

You'd think the boys would tease, but they don't. He's that dear. One of the MacAlister boys, Harper, calls him his sweetheart.

A thing I don't hold with is one person telling another how to lead their life, like with the neckties and the two preachers. They say the half the flock that holds with Holroyd are going to build another church right across the highway.

What, Leon? Of course we're mountain people. He says mountain people have always lived the way they want to. Leon *will* sit in the car and talk to the dashboard while I'm selling produce.

Lattimer, now, wants a gingham dress he saw in the window of Lesser's uptown. Why, I said, all I need is a yard and a half of gingham off the bolt at Woolworth's, some rickrack for the collar, a card of buttons, and I can sew one just like it. Pleats and all. I've used the pattern many's the time, for Sue Elizabeth's red dress she wears to school for one, Maddie Mae's pink dress for another.

What, Leon? Leon says it's cheaper than a pair of overalls. That's true. Well, I guess that's it. What say, Lattimer? It's not polite to whisper, I've always heard. What? Lattimer wants you to know he thinks your permanent wave is becoming.

Yes, Leon, we're through.

BADGER

Baltic Sailor

Into Scoresbysund seamed with frost and blue with hindered green, the brave sails of Erik Nordenskiöld; into the yellow hills and red villages of the Medes, Tobias, his dog, and the archangel Rafayel; into Nørreport, by train from Kongens Lyngby, Allen. Badger was waiting for him in the station lavatory, laughing at his cleverness in being there.

—What a bog, Badger said. My, you're handsome, as boys go, and you've come off without the cello and the Telemann sonata in four movements you've practiced all week. Thorvaldsen says that he gets lots of fife-and-drum stuff from the Lutheran Sodality Marching Band, and unseemly hornpipes and rock and roll from around on Nyhavn, but has never heard the kind of recital we give on Amagertorv. Very superior cat, you understand, is Thorvaldsen, and always has the church organ and string quartets to drop mention of when I brag about your street concerts on the cello.

Allen flicked off the blue ascot his mother made him wear to go with his eyes, and poked it into his haversack. Then he pulled his shirt over his head, replacing it with a gray sweatshirt from the haversack. Next he exchanged his short pants for exiguously shorter ones, the zipper of which did not go all the way up.

—Barepaw, too? Badger asked.

—No underwear, either, friend Badger.

—I assume, then, Badger said while offhandedly rooting at a flea, that you being twelve years old and all, and the cello nowhere in sight, and Edna not along, we don't allude to this outing back home?

—I don't think so, no. We're only out to learn a thing or two, anyway. No big deal.

—No no, of course not. I see we're going to put the haversack into the locker, to be retrieved on the way back. You think of everything.

—Not exactly in diapers still, you know.

Badger laughed, as he loved a conspiracy. He loyally did not ask where they were going. He would find out.

White Prairie Aster

I long ago lost a hound, a bay horse, and a turtledove, and am still on their trail. Many are the travelers I have spoken concerning them, describing their tracks and what calls they answered to. I have met one or two who have heard the hound, and the tramp of the horse, and even seen the dove disappear behind a cloud, and they seemed as anxious to recover them as if they had lost them themselves.

English Stonecrop

—If, Badger remarked on Gothersgade, we go into the Rosenborg Have we'll see naked girls sunbathing.

—*Ork jo!* Allen said. Later. First, we're going to the botanical garden.

—Because I'm home asleep on your bed, and dogs aren't allowed, as we chase the ducks and make the grebes nervous, and are cheeky to the swans?

—*Tetigisti acu.*

—Plautus. But why the botanical garden? Greenland wildflowers. You like those. Ghost of Hans Christian Andersen in the hothouse, upside-down over the begonias, legs opening and closing like scissors.

—To sweeten my dare with delay.

—Oh, that.

Fish

In Hendrik Goudt's engraving, Tobias, lugging the fish, steadied by Rafayel, is crossing a stream on stepping stones. Nimrod, the dog, is gathering himself to jump to the next stone as soon as Rafayel's foot is out of the way. There are oxen on the far side of the stream. Two frogs, who must soon stretch themselves into elastic leaps or be trod on, to their way of thinking, by a twelve-year-old, an angel, and a dog, having no way of knowing that Rafayel is weightless and must move, step by step, as if he were a mass responding to gravity, get set to jump. The sky, above lush trees, has clouds and geese.

5

Peter Freuchen, brushing frost from his beard, brought the wall of ice between the black sea and a black sky close enough in his binoculars to see the long grooves of exact crystal that wrinkled its surface.

Baltic Sailor

The stranger facing Allen was blond and trim. His intense gaze made the blue discs of his eyes seem slightly crossed. His shirt sleeves were rolled above his elbows. His jeans were pleated with creases across the top of the thighs and at the knees. Twenty, friendly, made in Scandinavia.

Red-beaked Grebe

In 1653 or thereabouts Rembrandt bought a plate by Hercules Segers, of Tobias and the angel Rafayel and the dog Nimrod. He changed it to a Flight into Egypt. Tobias became Joseph, Rafayel Mary, and Nimrod the donkey.

—And, said Badger, in Moses van Uyttenbroeck's picture Nimrod is barking at ducks and scaring them off the lake.

—Tobias and Rafayel are both twelve in that, and Tobias is dragging the fish.

—Yes, but this is in the Bible. Why does Nimrod get to worry ducks, and in a civilized and most advanced country like Denmark dogs can't go near the duck pond without being shouted at by the constabulary?

—What you see, you know, Allen said, you own. You take it in. Everything's an essence. Papa, you remember, when I was explaining this to him, said that at twelve you understand everything. Afterward, you have to give it up and specialize.

—Ducks are not to be believed. Give up coherent light for articulate light. Puppies understand everything, too, and then have to get a job looking after twelve-year-olds in downtown København with no shoes or socks, smitch of pants with lazy zipper, and a pullover shirt as might be worn by the bucket boy on an eel trawler.

—The film of essences, one photon thick, is continuous. Everything apprehended is in the continuum of this film. So all correspondences, the relation of information to other information, are first of all differences. Colors, shapes, textures. Quit yawning. This is important.

—It rather tried your papa's patience, didn't it, until you said that the great thing is affability, not the kinship but the kindness of one thing to another.

—And Mama remarked what a sweet pagan she had for a son.

—Edna stuck out her tongue.

—*You* sighed and whuffed.

8

Because they, too, were his, the lilac arbor and beds of Greenland wildflowers blue and yellow, Allen walked with studied idleness along the dappled paths of the botanical garden, his dare to himself prospering with delay.

—Getting your courage up, aren't you? Badger asked while looking with slitted eyes at a swan. You could be on roller skates, in your spatter jeans. You could be eating pea pods in Gray Brothers. You could be into the second movement of the Telemann.

—I have things to learn.

—The caterpillar of the codling moth feeds on the kernels of apples and pears.

Kierkegaard in the Trollwood

The stranger facing Allen was blond and trim. His intense gaze made the blue discs of his eyes seem slightly crossed. His shirt sleeves were rolled above his elbows. His jeans were pleated with creases across the top of the thighs and at the knees. Twenty, friendly, made in Scandinavia.

Crickets in Flixweed

An aristocracy of swans pushed haughtily through a commonality of ducks and a yokeldom of grebes.

—When a buck flea backs up, scrunched in, to jump, I snip the tickle, he jumps, I snap, he bites, I snick. Fuckering flea.

On a path that curved through deep lilies and high shrubbery, Allen, eyes hypothetically sneaky, lips puckered in supposition, unzipped, as if to pee, as might be. The school nurse, a good sort, had looked at it during his last physical, with an amused smile, and winked. Harald's had a callus on it, and looked bruised, like Papa's.

—With friendly numbers, Badger said, the divisors of the one add up to the other. The example given by Pythagoras is two hundred twenty and two hundred eighty-four.

—Cold nose, Allen said. Bugger off.

—The divisors of two hundred twenty are one two four five ten eleven twenty twenty-two forty-four fifty-five and one hundred ten, and they add up to two hundred eighty-four, which is the number friendly to two hundred twenty. Now you can't get it back in your pants, can you?

—A friend is another self, like the friendly numbers two hundred twenty and two hundred eighty-four. Didn't think I was listening, did you?

—And the divisors of two hundred eighty-four add up to two hundred twenty.

—So what does it mean, O Badger?

—That as many ways as one friend can be divided sum up to the other. Better stuff your dick back in, there's somebody coming. You smell as if you were with Harald eating chocolate and listening to a Bach partita.

—Looks like big business hard in my pants, wouldn't you say?

—Oh, absolutely. Hate fleas. You're a handsome boy.

—You're a handsome dog.

—The lion in the zoo is a cat who's a dog. Monkey is a dog who's a spider.

Ohio Bee, Ohio Honey

I long ago lost a hound, a bay horse, and a turtledove, and am still on their trail. Many are the travelers I have spoken concerning them, describing their tracks and what calls they answered to. I have met one or two who have heard the hound, and the tramp of the horse, and even seen the dove disappear behind a cloud, and they seemed as anxious to recover them as if they had lost them themselves.

12

Mellow gold and muted silver, a bed of flowers. Harald's scoutmaster says that a disposition to fall in love makes everybody look good. The truly beautiful, like Harald, don't need rationalizing, but you can think of a hooked nose as kingly and a snub nose as cute and a rough complexion as masculine and a sallow face as sensitive.

—That's Plato, Badger said. Is it for Harald that we're here in the botanical garden wondering how the divisors of a friendly number add up to the components of its friend? What we have are differences containing samenesses. Differently distributed. That's nicely tricky, *jo*?

Yellow Willows Along a River

To tune his ears to the hearing of Tobias, Rafayel discovered with cunning questions that human beings cannot hear the roaring fires of the stars or thunder on the wanderers or the hiss of winds across space. Nor could they hear the creak of trees growing, the tread of ants, or the rumble of seedlings breaking ground to stand in light.

14

—Thorvaldsen down on Sankt Annæ Plads likes to be called *Your Grace*, like his person the bishop.

—You're a funny dog, Badger, to like cats.

—Why not? He's fun to talk to. Cats don't like dogs because we smell butts and they resent it. They smell mouths, did you know? Anyway, I get along with His Grace Thorvaldsen the Holstein cat. They know things, cats. Their ear is more critical than a dog's. Good nose, too, but the whole race of them is so prudish and inhibited as to seem to have no nose at all. Did you know that the bishop's parish includes Greenland? I was telling him about you and Harald leapfrogging each other the whole length of the Købmagergade, and he began to brush his chest and inspect his paws.

—The boys we saw when we were coming from the station, Allen said, copperknob and towhead, who were sharing a Coke at a small table in that sandwich shop.

—Towhead's hair is very grebe chick, Badger said. We were supposed to take it for punk, wouldn't you say? You envy them their one Coke, age, and decisively creased jeans.

—Do I, now?

—Oh yes. You and Harald don't have to share a Coke. You each have your own.

—I'd rather share.

—Are you in love with Harald?

A duck belonging to the Rosenborg moat was crossing the Gothers-gade, halting traffic.

—Probably, Allen said.

—Is that a good thing or a bad?

—Good, I'd say. Very good.

—Well, then.

—Precisely.

—Headed for the Rosenborg Have, are we?

—Why not, friend Badger?

—Why not, indeed.

Tent Interior by Lantern Light

A stout wind fell on them from the north. Their tent tried to fly away before they could peg it to the forest floor. The rain, fine and swiveling, began when the tent was almost trig and their gear was half unpacked. They were inside, Harald and Allen, snug and with the lantern lit, when the rain began to blow sideways.

—Nothing neater, Harald said. Off our clothes.

—We'll freeze.

—Into dry, I mean, until dossing down.

—Sardines, crackers, cheese, chocolate milk.

—Coffee in the thermos, as filled at Rungsted Kro. Socks.

—What about socks?

—To hang above the lantern. First, to sniff. Me, yours, Olaf does.

—Here. Jesu Kristus, you really are. Like Badger.

—Nice. Thing is, to know the person you like. Olaf talks about the secret and privileged smells. Shirt.

—Wouldn't get me anywhere to be embarrassed, would it?

—Everything smells like lilac.

—Jasmine. Body oil, after my bath. And sweat from hiking all day.

—Body oil.

—Keeps my skin from drying out and itching.

—What a baby you are, still. Briefs.

—Briefs. Soon as I get them off. Am I to copycat? What do I sniff for, if I sniff?

—Put me a sardine and a bite of cheese on that cracker. Olaf sniffs to drive himself crazy, he says. But he's lovely crazy to begin with. Makes his wizzle stand, all twenty centimeters.

—And then what?

—Listen to the rain.

16

Drum and fife! The Queen's Guards were marching from the barracks in ranks of three, files of ten, in busbies and blue, musettes on their butts, their sergeant-major strutting to *There Is a Tavern in the Town*.

Scholar with Lion and Pot of Basil

The stranger facing Allen was blond and trim. His intense gaze made the blue discs of his eyes seem slightly crossed. His shirt sleeves were rolled above his elbows. His jeans were pleated with creases across the top of the thighs and at the knees. Twenty, friendly, made in Scandinavia.

Time Sinks in Orion

A girl with pink nipples and high hard breasts was taking off her jeans in the Rosenborg, among as many sunbathers as seals on an Aleutian beach. A triangle of arcs, her *slip*, flag red, and her friend with a swimmer's back and saucery hollows in his solidly boxed buttocks was cupped into a gauze pouch and cingle. Their mouths were grazing each other's lips in slow circles, their jeans still around their ankles. Badger trotted over to smell.

—Kelp and olive, his, he said, laughing. Tuna and mayonnaise, hers.

— You're awful, you know, pal Badger. You belong to a different order of being.

—Dog, part lion, part wolf. When you and Harald swapped underpants, you sniffed his before putting them on.

— They smelled of clean laundry, with a whiff of hay-mow.

19

Hillside thick with meadow flowers, midges, butterflies, gnats, a wall of Norway pines on the other rim of the dip, an empty sky, a lonely place rich in silence, in remoteness, in stillness. He and Harald, piecemeal naked by the time they'd got to the middle of the slant field, shirts over their shoulders, sneakers untied, suddenly looked at each other, serious with surmise and then all monkey grins. Best of friends, Harald. He was naked first. They lay in dense grass, gazing up into the absolute August blue.

—There's snug, Harald said, hand straying, like our tent that rainy night in the forest.

—Slushy inside, too, like drenched, sperm from chin to knee.

—And there's open, like here, where you can see to the top of the sky, and in all directions. There's nowhere as private as the middle of a field.

Dutch Sky Piled with Clouds

Tobias carried the fish, which would have been too heavy for him except that Rafayel made local adjustments in gravity. A sparrow flew right through Rafayel. Only Nimrod noticed. They did not walk on Shabbat.

Flanders Under Rain

I long ago lost a hound, a bay horse, and a turtledove, and am still on their trail. Many are the travelers I have spoken concerning them, describing their tracks and what calls they answered to. I have met one or two who have heard the hound, and the tramp of the horse, and even seen the dove disappear behind a cloud, and they seemed as anxious to recover them as if they had lost them themselves.

22

Log cabin, Troll Wood Troop, Danish Free Scouts. Olaf, a fall of hair over one eye, sitting on a picnic table, legs crossed, had told them about Janusc Korczak and King Matthæus.

A long silence. Harald's arm across Allen's shoulders. Benjamin asked about Poland, the Nazis, the war. Aage asked why the sky is blue, and why it's bluest in August. Rasmus said that it was bluest in October, and wanted Olaf to tell them again about the inner parts of girls, exactly what was going on there. Isak wanted to hear more about the Education No Thanks kids in Düsseldorf, who ran a bicycle shop and defied all authority, settled enemies of capitalism, the family, and girls. Ejnar invited everybody to join him in a swim in the inlet, before the Swedes poured ice water into the ocean, as was their wont about this time of day, and was seconded by Marcus, who was already naked. Hjalmar offered to march them to the inlet with Haydn on his horn, Hommel on his drum.

Allen was most interested in a naked Olaf, about which he'd heard so much from Harald.

—It is sort of unbelievable, he whispered in Harald's ear.

—What's unbelievable? Marcus asked, loud.

—Who else, Ejnar crowed through the shirt he was pulling over his head, marches to a swim with a French horn and drum as spiffy as the Queen's Guards? Style is what we have, that's what.

—Watch, Harald said to Allen.

He bounced, with turns on his heel, over to Olaf, who lifted him onto his shoulders, with an awesomely squeezed hug on the way up. Harald was radiant, Olaf complacent.

Later, winded and dripping, Hjalmar and Hommel wrestling like puppies in the sand, Olaf said that he and Harald and Allen were going to walk back to the cabin the long way round, through the woods on the slope. Was Allen, Olaf asked when they were having a pee in the wood, comfortable with the outing, with the troop, with Harald?

—Oh yes. Sure.

—Allen only looks timid, Harald said. His heart's a lion's, a lazy lion's.

—Thanks, Allen said. Badger will like that.

—Who's Badger? Olaf asked.

—Allen's dog. Is he here, Allen friend?

—Not yet.

—How, Olaf asked, could a dog get here if Allen didn't bring him?

—Easy, Harald said. I've been on long bike rides with Allen when Badger was along, though all I could see, not being as spooky as Allen, was the empty air. I sometimes think, though, that I've felt Badger's Alpo breath and got a whiff of his dogginess. And Allen smells like Badger if you get him before a bath.

Olaf, confused, had other things on his mind. He had taken a course in modern art with Allen's mother at the university.

—And your father edits a classics journal, doesn't he?

—I think so, Allen said. Something like that. Wait till I tell Mummy one of her students is Harald's scoutmaster.

—She'll have to sit down, I imagine, Harald said.

Badger

Of pests, the flea the fly the tick the leash, none stings like want, when you are not there, where you are not then. The box on rounds the two legs roll in, its stink is not worse than being here when Uln is there. What are mustard, Ejnar? And Swan Wings with the ozone midnight smell and Tobias who smells like Harald and Nimrod their dog whose real name is Wind and with them a Fish. With ducks there are three, duck and drake and the drake's drake friend Anders. Not natural for them not to fight but what do ducks have for brains? Uln smells good when he's with Harald, and feels good, so we like Harald.

24

Allen's suspicion that people created themselves was the only way he could explain Olaf. His parents could not have designed him. Parents don't think that way. God? But why would God, whose thoughts are pure, have curved Olaf's upper lip just that way, with the tuck and dimple at the corners, and shaped him all over in such a cunningly sexy and perfect a style that everything about him was the way Allen also wanted to be. Truth was, and why do people not say this, Olaf made himself. You have to know what you want to look like. Nature complies.

—It sounds right, you know? Harald agreed. You've found something out. But Olaf's body comes from swimming and running and the gym.

—Understood, friend Harald. But his smile and the look in his eyes and his friendliness don't. How did he get those? And everybody has a cock, all boys I mean, but Marcus's looks like a grub and his balls are peanuts.

—Olaf's seventeen, Marcus ten.

—Can you believe that Olaf's looked like Marcus's when he was ten? Never. I'd say it was the size of a *polser* and stuck out, like yours, admired by all. Olaf thought his cock into the handsome monster it is.

—I know that he had a friend when he was little. He told me. Never needed to say they wanted it. They knew at the same time. Dropped their pants together, as if there'd been a signal. I think Olaf's been sad since then. The friend got a whiff of girl around fourteen and has been on them, in them, since, humping away, with just enough wits left to stagger around between fucks. Olaf says girls are all wrapped up in themselves, hard to make friends with.

The Red Villages of the Medes

Rafayel discovered that he could talk to Nimrod more easily than to Tobias.

—The grief of the fish, he said.

—Dun clouds on a Friday, Nimrod said. A flame is fat with sinking while it is slender with rising.

—The wife of four is three.

—Nine is the grandmother of numbers.

—Walking, Rafayel said with wonder in his voice, walking. There were trees of crows at Charleville, a winter of crows. Or will be. Tenses are not for angels. A boy named Jean Nicholas Arthur. Like Tobias. Like Uln. I walked, will walk, walk with him toward black trees in a winter field, the angelus chiming from the square tower of a small church, the rim of the world red where it was rolling away from your star. He spoke of the Prince of Aquitaine, whose heart was widowed and dark, and cried *Give me back Pausilippe and Italian sea!* and the crows cried in their hundreds *The sun is dead!* The wind carried their caws.

—The wind, Badger said.

—The wind, said Allen.

—One hundred crows!

—What does a dog know?

—Ask Nimrod. He knew that Rafayel was not people, by his smell. No oniony armpits, only celestial electricity, rich in ozone. Thorvaldsen, now, would have taken Rafayel to be a higher rank of bishop, and from Sweden. He would have stropped his leg. He would have sat across from him on an episcopal cushion, pretending to be of equal rank among ecclesiastical cats.

Scoresbysund

The stranger facing Allen was blond and trim. His intense gaze made the blue discs of his eyes seem slightly crossed. His shirt sleeves were rolled above his elbows. His jeans were pleated with creases across the top of the thighs and at the knees. Twenty, friendly, made in Scandinavia.

27

—Of course I made myself! Olaf said. Allen's right as rain. How plain I used to be, I won't say. Around three, it must have been, sucking my thumb, knock-kneed, and given to whooping cough, nose drip, and pyromania, I began to rethink myself. By six, still a thumbsucker, I had a vision. I knew that I admired some people and found others revolting. Being a philosopher, I knew that the people I didn't like were being repulsive on purpose. There was a girl with a kind of pearly mole just inside her nostril. She had made it grow there, to annoy her parents, and me. She liked to puke in Kindergarten, without warning. Nurse asked her one hundred times at least to point to her mouth when she was going to barf. She never did. Oh, the happy beam in her eyes when she had spattered her coloring book, my blocks, Nurse's shoes. So it followed that the people I loved had made themselves adorable. By eight I was in love to the point of being legally insane with a twelve-year-old who had big brown eyes and a mop of curls, and long legs, and petted his crotch in public. I would willingly have died if I could have *been* him, if only for one day. I did the next best thing: I set out to wish myself, will myself, magic myself, to be him. This worked. It worked so well that when I met Hugo at twelve, he was in love with me, I discovered with my heart floating up to my mouth. That should happen to everybody at least once. We became each other. Wore each other's clothes. There's a pair of little denim pants I have packed away, thin as gauze and threadbare, which we both wore.

Wind Around a Corner, Full of Leaves

I long ago lost a hound, a bay horse, and a turtledove, and am still on their trail. Many are the travelers I have spoken concerning them, describing their tracks and what calls they answered to. I have met one or two who have heard the hound, and the tramp of the horse, and even seen the dove disappear behind a cloud, and they seemed as anxious to recover them as if they had lost them themselves.

29

The first night Allen spent at his house, Harald as soon as his folks left for a dinner party walked around naked in the back garden, level sunlight making gold fire in his hair.

Park with Figures

A young man lay as if fallen from the sky onto the grass of the Rosenborg greensward, arms and legs spread, his shirt rolled under his neck, jeans open and briefs pushed onto his hipbones.

—I would like, Badger said, to be the drum major in front of the Queen's Guards when they're marching to *The Stars and Stripes Forever*, and I'd love to roll in horse flop and not get lectured on it. Also, I'd like to visit a jungle, for the tremendousness of it, you know? But you're looking at that boy with hair all but down over his eyes and his underpants bowed out in front. Butterflies, monkeys, frogs, shelf fungus, green fleas, sponge trees, blue parrots, yellow parrots, red parrots, and vines as long as Jylland if you straightened them out.

—The principle of essences, Allen said, is identity: each essence's being is entirely exhausted by the character which distinguishes it from any other essence. It's for Harald we're here, O Badger.

—Taking things in, Badger said, that's what's important. Your mother said so. Said that if she could teach her children to miss nothing of what the world has to give, she would be doing her duty. Her example, you remember, was a pear tree in bloom. We're being admired.

—I am, anyway. What do you suppose she means?

—Got me. The rock dove flits starbright through the oleanders.

—Amber gleam, Allen whispered, of the wild partridge in umber gloom. I can recite poetry, too. He is staring at me, isn't he?

—A pear tree in bloom. *Ork jo.*

—White, fragrant, green, by a brick wall, beside a roof, thatched or tile, pears to come, if fuckered properly by bees. Lovely in sunshine, rain, moonlight. Crisp blossoms in profusion, small, tender, white.

—Painted by Stanley Spencer.

—Christian Mølsted.

—Charles Burchfield.

—Samuel Palmer.

—Hokusai.

—I forget that I'm invisible, not here to be seen.

—Brave's the word.

—Don't you think your admirer's a bit rough, from the Christianhavn docks, wouldn't you say?

—I would say that, yes.

—Dirt under his fingernails. Good-looking, though. Flat bone down his nose, plumb from where his bronze eyebrows almost join, to the square tip. What does Telemann *mean* in the slow movement?

A Ruckling of Doves

The high wall around the yard was grown over with Virginia creeper, which a breeze tickled. Trees beyond the wall, lazily liquid in the fitful wind that precedes rain, were so tall and densely green that the yard was a square space in a thick forest. Allen studied a compass, an ordnance map. He made a study of the sky, Baltic blue marbled yellow and green.

The house was still, empty. The ladder was against the wall. A wheelbarrow. A rake. A hamper basket.

He knelt to untie his sneakers, stood on one leg, and then the other, to pull off his socks.

Harald toward dawn in the tent had said that the rain, with them so warm and close, was the finest sound he had ever heard.

The clouds were drifting from the east. He tugged his jersey over his head and rolled it into a baton.

Next it rains, she had said, if you could believe girls. He believed Hanna. She had freckles, wore glasses, and knew things. She was witty, but nice, about Harald. So that was all right.

He took off his shorts and wrapped them around his rolled jersey. Red underpants. Did the sun make fire in his hair as it had in Harald's? You are the earl of the elves, Hanna had said. Not passed on to Harald, who would flip his fingers. Lord of the forest. Telemann, the slow movement, and rain on the tent.

The Sedge to the Sea

How did Badger know where he was going, that he could accurately run ahead? Harald liked to be sniffed by Badger, reveled in it. Boys, Edna said, are so thick, you can't find a place where you could shove in a pin. And Badger was comically confused when Harald passed over the frayed, worn denim pants Olaf lent him with the injunction that if he lost them, or tore them, he'd wish he was somebody else in another country. But had wanted us to wear them.

—But we do understand, Harald had said, ever so seriously.

—I hope so, Olaf said. I'd hate for me and Badger to be the only ones here who see what's going on.

—I'll tell you, Allen said. It's like the day I finally took Badger into town with me, so his curiosity could be satisfied. He was out of his mind happy, looking at everybody, everything. And when he saw how I make a territory on Strøget, all mine, all ours, he almost wagged his tail off with pleasure, and when I set up the music stand and played, he too was playing the cello, and acknowledging every attention, beating time with his tail to a music none of us will ever hear.

—Don't we? Harald said.

—If, Harald, Olaf said, you hadn't said that, I would have been disappointed the rest of my life.

Into Nørreport

I long ago lost a hound, a bay horse, and a turtledove, and am still on their trail. Many are the travelers I have spoken concerning them, describing their tracks and what calls they answered to. I have met one or two who have heard the hound, and the tramp of the horse, and even seen the dove disappear behind a cloud, and they seemed as anxious to recover them as if they had lost them themselves.

Wo es war, soll ich werden

I

—See? Pascal said, handing Housemaster Sigurjonsson a bunch of chicory and red valerian, they're flowers, for you, because Franklin brings them to Hugo Tvemunding, who puts them in a jar of water and says he likes them. They're sort of from the edge of fru Eglund's garden.

—So will I put them in a vase, Holger said, if I have such an article. Which I absolutely don't.

—The marmalade, Pascal said, is down to just about enough to go on a slice of bread, with some butter, and then you'd have that to put the flowers in. Hugo keeps pencils in a marmalade jar.

—Ingenious solution, Holger said. And who do we know fossicking for tucker to finish off the marmalade with a cup of tea, perhaps?

—Milk, a big glass of cold milk. There's half a bottle and one not opened yet. You've been grading papers, all done, with the rollbook on top and a rubber band around the lot. And reading. Saw you at the gym.

—Danish grasses and wildflowers, the papers, Holger said. And what in the name of God is that?

Pascal, eyes as wide as kroner, was wiping marmalade out of the jar with his fingers.

—Sounds like somebody's mad at somebody, he said.

His sandwich built of wedges of butter and runnels of marmalade, Pascal took as large a bite as he could, for the comedy of it, accepting a tumbler of milk from Holger.

—One of 'em's Franklin, he said, cocking an ear.

His smile gilded with marmalade and wet with a chevron of milk, Pascal eased down the zipper of his fly: his accompanying Holger on bed-check rounds every evening was always in night attire, pert briefs with a snug pitch to the cup.

The ruckus down the hall became fiercer. What Holger saw when he whipped open his door and sprinted out was Franklin Landarbejder and Adam Hegn, whose tenor insults and shoulder punches had exploded into a locked scuffle, pounding each other in white hate. Falling in a flail-ing crash to the floor, they were rolling, kicking, caterwauling, elbowing and biting along the corridor floor like a bearcub attacked by a hive of bees, trying all at once to tuck itself into a ball while thrashing out at its stinging tormentors.

The first out of his room was Asgar with a yellow pencil between his teeth.

—Knee him in the balls, he said. Buggering Jesus, there's blood.

Tom, pulling on shorts that snagged on his erection, poked a bare foot into the grunting ferocity, trying to pry Franklin's elbow away from Ad-am's throat.

Edvard with a calculator, Olaf in a white sweatshirt with *ungdoms-frihedskæmper* in blue lettering vertical from waist to collar, Bo stark na-ked.

—Go it, Franklin, Bo said. Go it, Adam.

—Back! Holger shouted, straddling the fighters and pulling them apart. Pascal, from nowhere, got Adam in an armhold and rolled him smack against the wall. Holger had pinned Franklin's arms, walking him back-ward. Adam was promising Pascal that he would kick the shit out of him as soon as he got the chance. Franklin shouted that Adam was the lover of his mother. Adam bled from his nose, Franklin from a cut lip.

—Tom, Holger said, get Matron. Pascal, fetch Hugo Tvemunding. Ed-vard and Olaf, take these outlaws to the infirmary. Where's Rutger? Jos?

Matron, in a bathrobe suggestive of the last imperial court in Peking and with hair improbably crisp for the time of day, lifted Adam and Franklin onto the examining table, side by side, where they sat glaring straight ahead. Adam she gave an ice cube in a twist of gauze to hold under his nose. Franklin she dabbed on the lip with a swab of iodine, commanding him to keep his mouth well open. Then she stripped them, had a thorough prodding look at their mouths, ears, eyes.

—No loose teeth, she said. Lucky, that. There will be bruises. I want to see you both again tomorrow afternoon. Animals, she added under her breath.

—Animal, Adam said to Franklin.

—You'd better believe it, Franklin said.

Adam, green, said he was going to barf. And did, into the gleaming stainless-steel basin Matron held under his chin with a magic pass.

—What precisely the fuck is all this? Hugo asked. Beg pardon, Matron.

—Fine example, Matron said, I must say. Onto your elbows and knees, Adam. Yes, on the table. Move down, Franklin. Breathe deep, relax.

—These two, Holger said, were mixing it in the hall. No great matter.

—End of the world, Mariana said. Look at them. I'm the blond rat's big sister, first certificate in nursing, St. Olaf's Day Care.

Matron smiled viciously.

—Ever so pleased.

Pascal, peeping around the door, got the full blast of a stare from Matron and disintegrated.

—Gotcha! Jos shouted, blocking, scooping up, heaving over his head, and catching Pascal hammocked knees and nape in his arms.

—Hoo! Pascal said, scare me out of a year's growth, huh?

—So look where you're going. What's in the nursery, shrimp?

Jos, Apollo in dirty white sweatpants rolled low on his narrow hips, hefted Pascal onto his shoulders.

—Franklin, Adam. They had a fight. Nosebleed, cut lip. Boy, do you stink. Hugo and Mariana have come over. Matron shot me with one of her looks.

—Working out. Adam's never even seen somebody like Franklin. To be beautiful. Is that your peter poking the back of my neck?

—Hugo's barefoot, fly's open and no underpants, and his sweater's on backward.

—Canarying in the bed with frøken Landarbejder, wouldn't you say, weasel?

—Look neither left nor right, Hugo said. Holger's rooms are at the far end.

—But if you look straight ahead, Mariana said, you see Tarzan in sweatpants held up by faith alone and with Pascal on his shoulders.

—Girl in the hallway! Bo called out.

Hugo guiding Franklin, Holger Adam, Mariana sorting and inspecting their clothes, deployed themselves around Holger's sitting room.

—Pascal! Holger called.

Mariana introduced herself to Adam.

—And just because I'm his sister doesn't mean that I'll take his side.

Pascal, wet and hugging a towel, said that here he was.

—I'm having a shower with Jos.

—Go get your dressing gown, for Franklin, would you, and Adam's, and be slippy, back here before I count ten.

—The things I'm learning, Mariana said.

The phone rang: the Headmaster.

—Tempest in a kettle, Holger said. We have the combatants, Tvemunding and I, here now. I'll give you a report. And a good evening to you, sir.

Pascal's dressing gown, the first Franklin had ever worn, was plaid, Adam's, soft with many launderings, Norwegian blue.

—A room to live in, Mariana said, work in, read in. Books by family and size, all these maps, good chairs, sheep in a pasture so nicely matted and framed.

—That's a Louisa Matthiasdottir, of an Icelandic meadow.

—Holger's an Icelander, Hugo said. I admire the Klee, glyphs of fruit and vegetables yellow and lavender on that blue ground. Two pears nuzzling. Apples, pears, cherries, and would that be a fig?

—Good botanist, Klee, accurate with structure.

—Where's Pascal's room? Mariana asked brightly.

While Holger was saying *really, I don't think you should,* she went out singing *Pascal!*

—Nosebleed would seem to have quit, Hugo said, but keep the ice under it a bit more, eh?

—Who cares? Franklin said.

—Enough out of you. And I don't want to hear an antiphony of *he started it.* Fights are things that happen. Gorbachev and Reagan do it with intercontinental ballistic missiles, you and Adam do it with fists and feet.

—He bit me.

—And teeth. It's ourselves we don't like when we think we don't like somebody. This unseemly fratch when you should have been doing your homework was Adam fighting Adam, Franklin fighting Franklin.

—He started it, Adam said.

Mariana came back peeping through her hands over her eyes.

—We'll take Franklin home with us, and Pascal too, for company. No war if the troops are restricted to barracks. Jos is very beautiful when he blushes from forehead to toes and everywhere in between.

—Here I am, Pascal said. Musette bag, see? Toothbrush comb jammies slippers and whichwhat. Had a shower. Jos says I look like a newt wet, an oiled elver. Uliginous eel I called him, ha!

—Wait till my parents hear about this, Adam said.

—Oh boy, Franklin said, searching the ceiling.

—You'll come over with us, Holger? Mariana asked.

—If I may. Let me set up a provisional government, with Jos in command, just in case this skirmish was the beginning of a revolution of sorts. Back in a sec.

—You look spiffy in Pascal's dressing gown, Beavertooth. We must get you one.

—I like it, Franklin said, solemn doubt in his voice.

—It's for the infirmary, Pascal said. You can have it.

Jos had followed Holger back, dressed in a towel knotted around his hips. A handsome smile for Mariana, a wink for Pascal, a sergeant's glare at Adam, a scout's salute for Hugo.

—Go on over, Hugo said, I'll be along. I want to hear Adam's side of this, just the two of us.

Adam said:

—We're not supposed to let outsiders in the dorm after six. I know he's a day student but that's an outsider 'sfar's the dorm is concerned. He gave me some sass, and, well, we got into it. I was following the rules. He doesn't belong here, anyway. He had no right to hit me.

—I couldn't agree more, Hugo said. And you were right to follow the rules. On the other hand, you knew perfectly well who Franklin is, and that he and Pascal are rather special friends. If I'd been in your place, I think I would have been less of a bufflehead, you know, and told Master Sigurjonsson (he was here) that Pascal had a visitor.

Stubborn silence, defiant eyes.

—So, Hugo said, this is really not my affair, it's Master Sigurjonsson's, and he's a good man, wouldn't you say? Jos is standing in for him for half an hour or so. Ho, Jos!

—*Adsum!*

He bounded down the hall and stood mother-naked at attention.

—All yours, lieutenant. I'm off. One wounded trooper here to cheer up.

With an easy hoist Jos heaved Adam butt up over his shoulder, about-faced with a military pivot and stomp, and strode along the hall.

—Node bleed! Adam squealed.

—What else? Hugo said. Carry on, corporal.

Mariana was making hot chocolate, Holger was looking the place over, holding his elbows, and Franklin was laying a fire, with a lecture for Pascal on how it's done.

—So this, Holger said, is Bourdelle's *Herakles the Archer.* I know everything here from Pascal's accounts. There's Tom Agernkop. What talent as a painter you have, Hugo. And the Muybridge.

—I like a bathrobe, Franklin said. It's like being in bed.

—World's coziest place, Mariana said. If ever I meet the art teacher who converted this over-the-old-stables upstairs into a studio apartment of such friendly privacy and then skedaddled precisely in time for Hugo to move into it, I'll give him a big hug and kiss.

—Continuous space, Holger said, and yet one can see that that's bedroom, this sitting room, and that kitchen, differences that are really distinctions in a sense of space. Whereas my rooms have walls and doors.

—Our bedroll goes here, Pascal said. Franklin calls it a pallet. In front of the fireplace. Camping out indoors: that's the fun of it.

—A bivouac of mice, Mariana said. Who wants marshmallows in their chocolate? Gerbils, maybe.

—No TV, but a radio, Franklin said.

A cork bulletin board to the right of the fireplace: a yellow-and-blue Cub Scout neckerchief, *museau de loup* and *fleur de lys* for insignia, a photograph of Pastor Tvemunding in a garden with Franklin polliwog naked by the hand, a map of NFS Grundtvig and its grounds, a dental appointment, a blue pennyweight *badebukser*, flimsy and nylon, lined housing of about a gill, a photograph of a frog and fieldmouse nose to nose, an embroidered shoulder patch for Wilderness Foraging (pine branch with cone), another for woodcraft (red hatchet on a buff ground), and one shoelace limp over a drawing pin.

—For having our chocolate on, Franklin said, lugging a sleeping bag from the closet, unrolling it along the hearth. I have Pascal's bathrobe, so he doesn't have one.

—Have Hugo's, Mariana said, fetching it. Woolly warm, modish slate gray with red piping and a red belt, only four sizes too large.

—Oh wow.

—Get in it bare-assed, like me, Franklin said.

—End of the summer, month before last, Pascal explained to Holger, we all went nude, except Pastor Tvemunding, at Hugo's cabin. I was embarrassed at first, but got used to it.

—In about fifteen seconds, Mariana said.

—Pastor Tvemunding was naked, too, I ought to say, when we had a dip in the ice-water pool of the ice-water forest stream. We bathed with him, and then Hugo and Mariana bathed, though we could bathe with them, too, and once we all had a bath in the pool together, as Pastor Tvemunding said water that cold made impure thoughts sheer folly.

—What in the world is this? Holger asked.

He had gotten up to walk around the room while Pascal stripped.

—A harmonium, Hugo said. For hymns.

He brought it over to the fire, explaining its workings, and put it in Mariana's lap.

—Stanford in A, he said. OK, rats, sweet and high.

Mariana began an updown-updown dactylic ground, vibrant and rich.

—*The Owl and the Pussycat*, Franklin sang.

—*Went to sea*, Pascal joined.

And together:

—*In a beautiful pea-green boat!*

Holger stood in charmed surprise at the beauty of their voices.

—*They took some honey and plenty of money*
Wrapped up in a five-pun note.

Franklin, off key, signaled for a pause until the melody came round again.

—Somebody's voice is changing, Hugo said in a deep bass.

—Go on! Holger pleaded. Go on!

—*The Owl looked up to the stars above,*
And sang to a small guitar,
O lovely Pussy! O Pussy, my love,
What a beautiful Pussy you are!

—*You are!* Mariana sang.

—*You are!* Hugo joined.

In quartet:

—*What a beautiful pussy you are!*

Franklin, sipping chocolate, slid his free hand up Pascal's nape and mussed his hair with wriggling fingers, and began the second verse.

—*Pussy said to the Owl, you elegant fowl,*
How charmingly sweet you sing!
O let us be married, too long have we tarried:
But what shall we do for a ring?

Mariana and Hugo:

—*They sailed away for a year and a day,*
To the land where the Bong-tree grows
And there in a wood a Piggy-wig stood
With a ring at the end of his nose.

Franklin:

—*His nose!*

Pascal:

—*His nose!*

Mariana, Hugo, Franklin, Pascal, and, hesitantly, Holger:

—*With a ring at the end of his nose!*

—Oh wonderful, Holger said.

Franklin's trying for a saucy pursing of his lips while he ran a hand down Pascal's back inside Hugo's roomy bathrobe ended in a grimace.

—Poor split lip, Mariana said.

Franklin shrugged: heroes don't complain.

—Instant retribution for wandering hands, Hugo said.

—Friendly hand, Pascal said.

Mariana, as if to change the subject, pranced a jig of chords on the harmonium, and began the third verse.

—*Dear Pig!* she sang. *Are you willing to sell for one shilling*
Your ring? Said the Piggy, I will.

Franklin and Pascal took over:

—*So they took it away and were married next day*
By the Turkey who lives on the hill.
They dined on mince and slices of quince,
Which they ate with a runcible spoon.

Hugo and Mariana:

—*And hand in hand on the edge of the sand*
They danced by the light of the moon.

Pascal, wild mischief in his eyes:

—*The moon!*

Franklin, feigning innocence:

—*The moon!*

All, with a sassy arpeggio from the harmonium:

—*They danced by the light of the moon!*

II

Blue Tent in a Grove of Birches

Once, God Almighty came to visit Adam and Eve. They welcomed Him gladly and showed Him everything they had in their house, benches and table and bed, ample jugs for milk and wine, the loom and ax and saw and hammer, and they also showed Him their children, who all seemed to Him very promising. He asked Eve whether she had any other children besides the ones she was showing Him. She said no. But the truth of the matter was that Eve had not yet got around to washing some of her children, and was ashamed to let God see them, and had pushed them away somewhere out of sight. God knew this.

Yellow Volkswagen

Holger Sigurjonsson liked to spend a night or two on weekends camping out alone, for the quiet, the peace of mind and soul, the integration of himself. He had said to Hugo that he was never busier than on these excursions, with nothing that had to be done except eating and sleeping. There was a keen excitement to the strategies of it all: packing precisely what was needed, choosing books to take along, discipline balanced to a nicety with freedom. He returned a much better person. I understand perfectly, Hugo said, and wish I had such talents. His camping out was with his scouts, or with Mariana and Franklin. Unity is at minimum two, and when Pascal had gone on an outing with Hugo and Franklin he came back radiant, less random in his conversation, which was famous in the school for moving without warning from the layered territories of a rain forest to the color theory implicit in choosing red socks to wear with a gray sweater. Hugo and Franklin, he reported, were friends of ever so interesting a psychology, for they were big brother and little brother without being kin, uncle and nephew, father and son (Pascal ticked these relationships off on his fingers), host and guest, and then there was something else which had to do with Franklin's being Mariana's brother.

4

Iceland is situated just south of the Arctic circle and considerably nearer Greenland than Europe, yet its plants and animals are almost wholly European. The only indigenous land mammalia are the Arctic fox (*Canis lagopus*) and the polar bear as an occasional visitor, with a mouse (*Mus islandicus*), said to be of a peculiar species. Four species of seals visit its shores. Ninety-five species of birds have been observed; but many of these are stragglers. There are twenty-three land, and seventy-two aquatic birds and waders. Four or five are peculiar species, though very closely related to others inhabiting Scandinavia or Greenland. Only two or three species are more related to Greenland birds than to those of Northern Europe, so that the Palaearctic character of the fauna is unmistakable. The Great Auk is now extinct.

Iceland

Dingy sheep in a meadow. Tall sky, banked clouds, through which shafts of glare. A yellow house.

Juck! Said the Partridge

Everything, Jos was saying to Pascal, Sebastian, and Franklin, can be done well. The art of eating an orange, watch. We want all the juice, *jo*? The long blade of your pocketknife, whetted truly sharp, with which we make a triangle of three neat jabs in the navel of this big golden orange picked by a Spanish girl with one breast jundying the other. Lift out the tetrahedral plug so sculpted. Suck. Mash carefully and suck again. Now we slice the orange into quarters, sawing sweetly with the blade, so there's no bleeding of juice. Like so, O puppy tails. One for each of us. Nibble and pull: a mouthful of tangy cool fleshy toothsome orange. And Sebastian has squirted his all down his jammies, the world being as yet imperfect. Eat a bit of the peel along with the pulp: not as great as tangerine peel, as preferred by God and several of the archangels, but still one of the best tastes in the world. Seeds and the stringier gristle into the trash basket.

Swallow the seeds and they'll grow an orange tree out of your ear. People who don't know how to eat an orange, like people who don't have the patience and cunning to pick all the meat out of a walnut, who don't eat peaches and apples skin and all, do not have immortal souls.

Harrat el 'Aueyrid

We removed again, and when we encamped I looked round from a rising ground, and numbered forty crater hills within our horizon; I went out to visit the highest of them. To go a mile's way is weariness, over the sharp lava fields and beds of wild vulcanic blocks and stones. I passed in haste, before any friendly persons could recall me; so I came to a cone and crater of the smallest here seen, 300 feet in height, of erupted matter, pumice, and light rusty cinders, with many sharp ledges of lava. The hillside was guttered down by the few yearly showers in long ages. I climbed and entered the crater. Within were sharp walls of slaggy lava, the further part broken down—that was before the bore of outflowing lavas—and encrusted by the fiery blast of the eruption. Upon the flanks of that hill I found a block of red granite, cast up from the head of some Plutonic vein in the deep of the mountain.

8

—Oh, I take him everywhere with me, Holger had said to Hugo. I can be brave enough to say that. Is that what you mean by imagination?

—No, Hugo said, that's love. Imagination's how you see him when he's with you. Because the Pascal you see isn't there, you know. That is, where Holger and Pascal maintain, you create in your imagination first a Holger, then a Pascal. That's why you're nuts about him: you like the imaginary Holger the imaginary Pascal brings into being.

—Is this something you're making up to be clever, Holger had asked, or could it be the reality of the matter?

—The reality, Hugo had said, is what you build on, a sprite of a boy with big intelligent gray eyes, crowded butterteeth, all that. No need to stammer and blush.

Pascal Studying His Toes

The hornbeam explains its leaves. Lays them out flat to the sun. Human honesty should do no less.

A Copperish Yellow Rose

In the summer of 1925, Mikhail Maikhailovich Bakhtin, the theorist of narrative, attended a lecture by A. A. Uxtomskii on the chronotope in biology. In the lecture questions of aesthetics were also touched upon.

Chicory and Red Valerian

The flowers Pascal had brought from the edge of fru Eglund's garden had been forgotten during the scuffle in the hall, and when Holger was leaving Hugo's, Pascal reminded him that the marmalade jar was to be washed and the flowers inserted.

—Put them, Franklin added, where they can eat some sunlight.

—A peculiar domestic event, Hugo said, cut flowers in a vase. Plutarch mentions the custom. A bouquet in among the dishes at dinner, and the diners wore garlands. I wonder if in a Greek house there were arrangements of flowers, on Plutarch's desk, for instance?

—Of course there were, Mariana said.

Coral Comb Dominicker Rooster

The soldierly carriage Holger had seen in Pascal of late he could trace to Franklin Landarbejder, whose spine at port arms and calves braced well back of a plumbline from knee to toe, square shoulders and high chin, parallel feet boxed in gym shoes of outsized sturdiness and socks thick as blankets, were the scoutly model. Trousers once chastely kneelength were now cockily short.

13

Hugo says that liking is not to be nattered at, Pascal said as he and Holger were walking in the long wood between the grounds and the river. He says there are two civilizations, one of the human in us, table manners, science, and such, and one of the animal in us. He says none of us is as good a human being as a dog is a dog, and this is because we're not good animals. He says Franklin and I like each other as animals like each other, two friendly dogs, say, and that he and Mariana like, he said *love* I think, each other as male and female animals, and she kicked him for saying this, but so that it was funny, you know. Franklin laughed, and Mariana said she'd always been able to see Franklin's long ears and tail and another word I didn't understand. But Hugo meant, he said, that we live in lots of ways at once, as animals and humans, and whatever our work is. Also, as doors that open onto things. A math teacher is a door opening onto math, a Christian is a door opening onto God. Something for others, and when he said this he made horns of his fingers above his ears and wiggled them at Franklin. But he wasn't talking to anybody in particular, that's what I like about him. Hugo just talks, to everybody or anybody.

Samovar with Lemon

The tall windows of the lecture room where Bakhtin heard Uxtomskii on the chronotope suffused a drab light upon rows of academic benches, the yellow oilcloth on rollers for diagrams and unfamiliar words, the lectern with kerosene lamp, water pitcher, and glass. One eye of Marx's bust was a pallid coin of light, the other a scoop of shadow. Holger was reading Bakhtin because he didn't understand narrative. Hugo had said that some French thinker held all understanding, especially self-knowledge, to be narrative in essence. A surprise, but there you were. A chronotope is the distinctive conflation of time and place fixing the Cartesian coordinates of an event or condition. Edward Ullman would have been interested, and Carl Sauer. The philosopher Samuel Alexander taught that finished time becomes a place. So every *where* needs a *when* in an account of it, and every event has a narrative past. Tvemunding, for all his dash, was up on everything, and Holger prided himself on following up. And here was a chronotope from ancient biology cropping up in a Russian book about narrative. The examples tended to be from Rabelais and Sterne, authors Holger had not read. Unlike the Russian lecture room remote in time and space, begrimed by poverty, political desperation, tedious idealism, his rooms at NFS Grundtvig were congenial and modern. The protocol was for the boys to knock and be invited in, or not, except for Pascal, who could enter when he pleased, always backing in with a double turn to close the door, a maneuver that maintained even if the door were open. One narrative might be to recall how it happened that Pascal fell into the habit of going with Holger on bed check, to ascertain room by room that everybody was in and accounted for. Pascal had once worn pyjamas on these rounds, as if to establish that he was ready for the evening, and Holger was sometimes in a dressing gown, sometimes in slacks, slippers, and tieless shirt. And as Pascal became accepted as Holger's familiar, as a teacher's pet whose transparent candor and chuckleheaded ignorance of privilege threatened no one, he began to imitate everybody else in the house by wearing briefs only, or a shirt only, for student by student God knew from day to day what, if anything, they would be wearing. Hugo was always in the know, and could answer why one style of undress had replaced another, or hairstyle, color of socks, brevity of underpants, snugness of jeans, the iconography of walls. Pascal's answers were unilluminating but current. Black socks were in, he would report. How did he know? Well, they just are. Papa's secretary is sending me some. So Mama will send me money for some. They duplicate everything.

15

There are no depths, Hugo had said, only distances.

16

—Rutger? Jos said.

He laid a protractor and compasses on graph paper nipped to a clipboard.

—He's on his knees and elbows out in the ferns jumping up Meg with sweet slick liquid shoves, and his tongue's down her throat, and his hot hands on her cool teats, having jittered her button until she was bucking. They're real friends, those two.

Holger, on bed check with Pascal in tow, sighed and smiled his patient smile. Asgar, reading on his bed, slid his hand inside his briefs.

—I know that problem, Pascal said, studying the clipboard.

—Psychologists and poets, Jos went on, are in the absolute dark about people like Meg and Rutger. They can be talking about Reagan and Gorbachev, Marilyn Horne and Pavarotti, Joyce and Kafka, and Meg's in there galvanizing his balls, mashing, petting, tickling, until she starts on his risen rosy pecker, giving little jumps, while he's groping in her panties until in the middle of Reagan and Gorbachev she's wagging her head like an idiot and Rutger's interspersing his remarks with whistles of appreciation, and they're both half in and half out of their clothes, a plump suntanned breast on view here for God and me to admire, a fine brace of balls there, a belly buckle, a healthy butt.

—You were there? Pascal asked.

—I'm not making this up, Jos said.

—Of course not, Holger said.

—And after they've made morons of each other, they resort to fucking as the only way back to sanity and this world, thumping like two rabbits.

—Ha! Pascal said, I've seen rabbits. The wife keeps chewing her lunch while the husband hunches her rear.

—Precisely, O infant friend, Jos said. And yes, I was not helplessly there, but there nevertheless. We were walking Meg back, I'd run into them and they insisted, so's I could walk back with Rutger, and we sprawled in the sun in the dell awhile. I'm used to their pawing each other, and they'd probably just screwed their brains sodden in Rutger's room after soccer practice. Anyway, once they've done Mr. and Mrs. Rabbit, they're themselves again, fresh as kittens after a nap. They give each other a silly look with deep eyes, find their underpants, brush off leaf trash, say hello to me, and start in on Reagan and Gorbachev again. One keeps one's cool with manly restraint. You hear that, Pascal? But exactly where Master Rutger is, I couldn't say.

17

The self, Hugo said, is the body. Our knowledge of what's other is a knowledge of our body. My seeing a Monet is a knowledge of my own eye, which is both an obstruction between me and the Monet and the medium by which I see it at all. If my eye is healthy and keen I can forget it. The self is invisible to itself when it goes economically about its real business. It is consumed in attention, and comes to being through attention. We do not watch our hand, nor yet the hammer, when driving a nail. We watch the nail. Reading, we see Robinson Crusoe with his parrot on his shoulder, yellow sands, green ocean, three goats on a knoll.

18

When Pascal and Franklin sang *The Owl and the Pussycat* to Mariana's accompaniment on the harmonium, Holger had blushed: thin wisps of tickling fire ran together deep inside him, surfacing on his cheeks and forehead, seeping back again, chill and stinging. Mariana gave him a merry look.

—Didn't half suck, did it? Franklin said.

—Did you like that? Pascal asked.

Holger's *Oh yes* was weak, and he blushed again. He took courage, and said that the old-timey tone of the harmonium made him remember hymns by lamplight in Iceland, his childhood.

—I must, he said, learn to read poetry.

—Join us, Mariana said. Hugo teaches me, and Franklin has to get yards of poems off by heart, Hugo's idea.

—Papa's, Hugo said. Once you know a poem, you have it for good.

Vesuvius

Standing from the morning alone upon the top of the mountain, that day in 1872 on which the great outbreak began, I waded ankle-deep in flour of sulphur upon a burning hollow soil of lava: in the midst was a mammel-like chimney, not long formed, fuming with a light corrosive breath; which to those in the plain had appeared by night as a fiery beacon with trickling lavas. Beyond was a new seat of the weak daily eruption, a pool of molten lava and wherefrom issued all that strong dinning noise and uncouth travail of the mountain; from thence the black dust, was such that we could not see our hands nor the earth under our feet; we leant upon rocking walls, the mountain incessantly throbbed under us: at a mile's distance, in that huge loudness of the elemental strife, one almost could not hear his own or his neighbor's voice.

A Bowl of Roses

Yellow kerchief, short blue pants.

—Roses? Holger said. I don't think I've ever really looked at one.

—Nor I, Hugo said. They are Italian opera, Austrian churches, German pastry. A proper flower is an aster, a daisy, a sunflower, something with decisive color and architecture.

—Precisely, Holger said. But Rilke's poem you say is superb, beginning with boys fighting, like Adam and Franklin, nasty little savages baring their teeth and hammering away at each other and rolling together like a bearcub attacked by bees. And then the poem goes on to be a description of a bowl of roses?

—*Die Rosenschale.* Anger flashing, two boys rolled themselves up in a knot of naked hate, tumbling over and over like some animal beset by a beeswarm. An outrage of going the limit. A cataract of runaway horses. Lips raised as if about to be peeled away. Rilke says he saw that, and I daresay he did, at military school where his father sent him after his mother raised him as a girl. Saw it and forgot it, he said, but obviously didn't forget it. Then the poem turns coolly to a bowl of roses. Like the battering boys they too occupy space. They are, they bend and open. They drink and digest light. They are boy and girl, stamen and pistil. Cool and ripe, their order of being is wholly beyond us, but we watch them as a lover watches his mistress. Inedible, they yet seem to belong with vegetables and fruit. But they belong to nothing but themselves, are nothing but themselves. Which means that, like us, like the pure being in us, they can take the outside in: wind, rain, the surge of springtime, shuffling chance and the inevitable, night, clouds running across the moon, on out to the most distant stars, can take all this and make an inwardness of it.

—I think I see, Holger said, but would hate awfully to be put on the spot and made to explain it. Fighting boys, roses in a bowl. Yellow roses, at that.

—The roses, Hugo said, are the boys. Where boys were, roses are.

—Lay that out flat, Holger said.

—Ha! said Pascal, coming to join them, to tie his shoelace, inspect his scuffed elbow, and look over his shoulder to see if Franklin was coming, too.

—When, Hugo said, I was a fetching spadger with rabbity teeth and big soulful eyes, out with my scout troop on a lake island, very rocky, cedary place, the air glittering with midges, I remember the heady, summery feel of it all, our scoutmaster undertook to instruct us in the facts of life.

—Facts of life, Pascal said.

—Twentyish, well built, he was a decent chap we all liked.

—By facts of life you mean sex, Pascal said.

—The very same, Hugo said, as set forth in a pamphlet. Which our competent scoutmaster consulted and followed. We sat in a half circle before him, slapping mosquitoes and waving midges away.

—Here I am, said Franklin, trotting up and leapfrogging Pascal's shoulders, a chaff of grass and leaves stuck to his short blue pants.

—We're hearing about long ago, Pascal said, Hugo's scoutmaster giving the facts of life to his troop.

—What for? Franklin asked.

—So, Pascal grinned, they'd know.

— *Voir est une science*, Hugo said. That's Jules Verne.

Pascal translated for Franklin, cupping hands over his ear and whispering.

—But, as I remember, it wasn't facts we were hungry for, but a sweeter knowledge. Not long before this I had been initiated by one Gretta into the mysteries of kissing, in rather a crowd of us who flocked to one house or another that was free of grown-ups for an afternoon or morning. Some of us were spies who reported the techniques of older brothers and sisters. Gretta knew about kissing in the manner of the French.

—Which is what? Franklin asked.

—Kissing open-mouthed and wiggling tongues together.

—Like you and Mariana. Icky, if you ask me.

— Yes, Hugo said, but what Holger and I were discussing at a philosophical level before we were joined by chirping mice in blue pants and yellow kerchiefs, is that knowledge is furtive and experimental, in the idiom of nature rather than that of diagram and axiom. A verb before it is a noun.

In any case, the facts of life were Gretta's kittenish tongue and hugs and caresses, which grew less tentative in the course of things. And there was the electrifying afternoon when, as we nudged each other to take a look, a look that made my mouth dry, Hjalmar Olsen, who was on hour-long French-kissing terms with three girls, all of whom were friends and compared notes and kept score, sneaked his hand into Charlotte Heggland's knickers, with her warm approval.

—Whee! Franklin said.

—So our lecture in a mist of midges lacked that grip on reality the young mind prefers to science from a pamphlet.

21

At afternoon, the weight of molten metal risen in the belly of the volcano hill (which is vulcanic powder wall and old lava veins, and like the plasterer's puddle in his pan of sand) had eaten away, and leaking at midheight through the corroded hillsides, there gushed out a cataract of lava. Upon some unhappy persons who approached there fell a spattered fiery shower of vulcanic powder, which in that fearful moment burned through their clothing and, scorched to death, they lived hardly an hour after. A young man was circumvented and swallowed up in torments by the pursuing foot of lava, whose current was very soon as large as Thames at London Bridge. The lower lavas rising after from the deep belly of the volcano, and in which is locked a greater expansive violence, way is now blasted to the head of the mountain, and vast outrageous destruction upward is begun.

Locker Room

—You have so many more resources, Holger said, as if nothing ever bothered you, a stranger to doubt.

—Doubt myself, you mean? Hugo asked, sifting talcum across his toes. Insofar as doubt's skepticism, I live from moment to moment doubting everything. You mean depression, which is the same as despair, a sin, you know. Despair is the enemy's most effective weapon. But despair is itself an enemy: the weapon makes the warrior. Except that depression, de-

spair, the feeling that everything's helpless, is not a warrior but a sneak behind the lines. His great lie is that things are necessarily so. All power
stands on the necessary despair of the ruled.

23

Before the morrow the tunnel and cup of the mountain had become a
cauldron of lavas, great as a city, whose simmering (a fearful earth-
shuddering hubbub) troubles the soil for half a day's journey all around.
The upper liquid mineral matter, blasted into the air, and dispersed mi-
nutely with the shooting steam, had suddenly cooled to falling powder;
the sky of rainy vapor and smoke which hung so wide over, and enfolded
the hideous vulcanic tempest, was overcharged with electricity; the thunders that broke forth could not be heard in that most tremendous dinning.
The air was filled for many days, for miles around, with heavy rumor, and
this fearful bellowing of the mountain. The meteoric powder rained with
the wind over a great breadth of country; small cinders fell down about
the circuit of the mountain, the glowing upcast of great slags fell after their
weight higher upon the flanks and nearer the mouth of the eruption; and
among them were some quarters of strange rocks, which were rent from
the underlying frame of the earth (5000 feet lower) upon Vesuvius, they
were limestone. The eruption seen in the night, from the saddle of the
mountain, was a mile-great, sheaflike blast of purple-glowing and red
flames belching fearfully and uprolling black smoke from the vulcanic
gulf, now half a mile wide. The terrible light of the planetary conflagra-
tion was dimmed by the thin veil of vulcanic powder falling; the darkness,
from time to time tossed aloft, and slung into the air, a swarm of half-
molten wreathing missiles. I approached the dreadful ferment, and
watched that fiery pool heaving in the sides and welling over, and swimming in the midst as a fount of metal, and marked how there was cooled
at the air a film, like that floating web upon hot milk, a soft drossy scum,
which endured but for a moment, in the next, with terrific blast as of a
steam-gun, by the furious breaking in wind of the pent vapors rising from
the infernal *magma* beneath, this pan was shot up sheetwise in the air,
where, whirling as it rose with rushing sound, the slaggy sheet parted di-
versely, and I saw it slung out into many great and lesser shreds. The pumy

writhen slags fell whistling again in the air, yet soft, from their often half-mile-high parabolas, the most were great as bricks, a few were huge crusts as flagstones. The poolside spewed down a reeking gutter of lavas.

Gym

Folding in, Holger said to Hugo, folding out. What one learns from the American geographers Ullman and Sauer is that if you really know anything, everything else comes into your subject. This is because, I think, you're on speaking terms with lots of other minds and consequently able to converse with yourself. I've often felt, you know, that I have not met parts of myself. I don't mean to be mystical. Scientific, rather, as the self in modern psychology seems to be a kind of averaging of several personalities.

25

Two raps on the door, Pascal with his complete turn on his axis, closing the door by backing against it. A bright look, as always, by way of hello. Holger, reading, gave his happy grin of welcome. Pascal took a deep breath, as of resolution, marched over with exaggerated steps, halted, heaved another resolute breath, and, leaning, kissed Holger on the cheek.
—Because, he said quickly, Franklin gives Hugo and Mariana a kiss when he comes in. Christians, way back, kissed when they met. Besides, Franklin said I should.

Laureldark Trailways

—Eglund, Hugo said to Holger, is all for drawing classes, and I threw in photography and printmaking as well while I had him in a good mood, and academic listings will soon sport an ad for a Grundtvig art teacher. Meanwhile, Jos jumped at the chance to sit for studies and an oil. And is right on time.

In floppy long sweatpants that rode low on his hips, so shallow in the seat that when he sat, as now, affable and open, the fact was shaped in compliant cotton soft from many launderings that he was the happy owner of two large testicles and a stout penis wide of rondure at the glans,

Jos looked from Holger to Hugo, Hugo to Holger, clowning pouts, smiles, and solemn faces.

—Off everything, Hugo said.

Jos peeled the tight tank top from the mounds of his pectorals, forced off his heavy gym shoes and thick socks, untied the drawstring of his pants, which he pushed to his ankles, and stood brown and naked, as unselfconscious as a dog. There was, near him, a spicily acrid musk, causing Holger to discover that Hugo always smelled of some expensive and far-fetched soap or gentlemanly lotion, lilac and cucumber, and that Pascal gave off whiffs of mown hay and peppermint toothpaste.

—You could take photographs of me, Jos said, and sell them in Copenhagen for God knows what.

With a merry smile for Holger, he asked if he were the chaperon.

—For me, not you, Hugo said.

—I'm here, Holger said, to see Hugo draw. I stand in awe of his talents. I was so wrongheadedly mistaken about him when he first joined the faculty, charming as he obviously was.

—Theology and classics mark a man, Hugo said. Here, Jos, put your weight on both feet, that's right, and cross your wrists on top of your head. I'll draw as fast as I can. As well as I can.

27

—I've been thinking about your question, which I answered so peremptorily, Hugo said, and thought you might have felt I was dismissing rather than answering it.

—Question? Holger asked.

—About Pascal and whether you might take him with you on one of your weekend camping jaunts.

—Oh, that, Holger said. I'm certain I shouldn't.

—I'm certain you should. You asked Franklin and me to take him camping with us, back in August. He enjoyed that immensely.

—And made friends with Franklin, who has caught his imagination.

—In a lovely way, Hugo said. As improbable a friendship as one can be, but decidedly one dropped down from heaven. I watch it with a measure of disbelief, learning more from it than any course in education I've

yawned and daydreamed through. Franklin, you understand, likes Pascal
for himself, as I think you do. What popularity Pascal has had has always
been for his brains, and maybe some for his sweet shyness, but I don't
think he's ever had a real friend. And Pascal adores Franklin for his
knuckly toughness. Genius and guttersnipe.

—I like your saying this, Holger said, because you understand my wanting Pascal to be happy, to have as many good things as he can. I'm as pro-
tective of him as I can be without drawing attention, which would make
him vulnerable in another way.

—But for yourself, Hugo said, you must take him on one of your weekends, lots of your weekends.

—Just the two of us?

—Just the two of you.

28

. —I did it! Mariana said. And I'm alive to tell it, and maybe even a bit
proud of myself. What's worse, I liked it!

—I who believe you can do anything, Hugo said comfortably from his
chair, am not surprised.

Holger, sitting with his arms on his knees, books and magazines
around his feet, scrambled up gentlemanly, startling himself in calling her
Mariana.

—I may, mayn't I? he asked.

—Lord, yes, she said, especially as I think I've called you Holger from the
start. What Hugo calls people, I do too. Fru Eglund, you remember, introduced herself from her garden, and said I must come to tea. Well, I've
been to tea with fru Eglund, telling myself that I've done braver things.
She's a sweet woman, you know? We talked flowers and curtains and
rugs, and then she got me to talking about the daycare center, and children, and then there was tea, which I didn't spill, or rattle my cup in the
saucer, and I really do believe, if I haven't dreamed it, that we pecked each
other affectionately on the cheek when I left.

—Wondrous and mysterious are the ways of God, Hugo said.

—And I didn't pee my knickers when Eglund himself came in and shook
my hand. *Stabilizing* he said you are, big Hugo. I swallowed my tongue

and smiled like an idiot. He said you're a stabilizing force at the school. And then he said a lot about your being a Christian in a bold and advanced way, and a solid classicist. Let's see what else he said. I was fogging over as he went on. Athlete, scoutmaster. Sensitive, responsible. Handsome young chap. And fru Eglund, she says I'm to call her Clarissa, said in a wonderfully motherly voice, Edward dear, I really don't think you need to commend doktor Tvemunding, *doktor!* to frøken Landarbejder. And *he* said, puffing on his pipe, my dear, everybody likes to hear good words about people they love, and I like to give people their just due. Clarissa said outside that I turned a sweet and becoming shade of pink. That's when I gave her a peck on the cheek.

—To understand all this, Holger, Hugo said, you have to know that Mariana hates all women.

—I do, Mariana said, they're cats. They have their heads up their behinds. I don't *believe* my mother. I've never had any girl friends. I prefer men, all of them.

She made Holger flinch by kissing him on the forehead. She kissed Hugo on the forehead, for symmetry's sake.

—Are Franklin and Pascal here? she asked. I need to hug them.

Sickle Sheen Flints

—Wolfgang Taute, Pascal said, says the Gravettian leaf points of eastern Europe, upper Paleolithic, got their tangs as they moved west, and became the willowleaf Swidry point. And probably were in touch with the Ahrensburgians.

—Tanged point technocomplex, Holger said. Reindeer people. The air blue with snow and ice splinters on long whistling winds that hit you like a plank. And in the summer, long marshes of yellow sedge.

Axiom

All problems, if ignored, solve themselves.

31

—Having talked more openly with you than with anybody in my whole life, Holger said, I'm willing to go along with you in this baring of bosoms.

I think you're trying to show me that I need to be liberated from something in myself.

—While keeping your privacy inviolable, Hugo said. I'm not prying. We've talked in abstractions. You were interested in Freud's enigmatic statement that *where it was, there must I begin to be.* The oyster makes a pearl around an irritant grain of sand. Nature compensates. A tree blown over will put out a bracing root to draw itself upright again. Deaf Beethoven composed music more glorious than when he could hear. Stutterers write beautifully. That is, one source of strength seems to be weakness.

—Surely not, Holger said. That sounds like the suspect theory that genius is disease: Mann's paradox. It's romantic science, if science at all.

—No no, Hugo said. Freud meant that a wound, healing, can command the organism's whole attention, and thus becomes the beginning of a larger health.

—Wounds in the mind Freud would have meant.

—Yes.

—I think, then, that I know what he means.

William Morris in the Faroes

These wild strange hills and narrow sounds were his first sight of a really northern land. The islands' central firth was like nothing he had ever seen. It was a place he had known in his imagination, mournfully empty and barren, remote and melancholy. In a terrible wall of rent and furrowed rocks, its height lost in a restless mist, he saw that the sublime can be hard and alien. There was no beach below the wall, no foam breaking at its feet. This gray land, without color or shadows, so fiercely defined as to mass of stone and harshness of detail, knew nothing of doubt, of the tentative, the gradual. Its geological decisions had been resolute. As his ship pitched and rolled toward the Icelandic coast, an eagle began to circle above them with plunges and rises of noble composure, wheeling wildly only when it was joined by a raven teasing and reproving. But both were free in the steep cold of a sky without barrier or restraint.

33

Outside his door, when Holger opened it, were Jos in a minim of sparely adequate briefs and Pascal gleefully piggyback.

—I'm delivering, Jos said, one gray-eyed toothy spadger, who has something to show you, and is about to explode.

—Holger! Pascal said, handing an envelope over Jos's shoulder, read it!

The long envelope bore the return address of the Royal Danish Geological Society and was to Professor Pascal Raskvinge. Inside was a letter accepting for publication Professor Raskvinge's paper comparing the geology of the Galapagos and Iceland.

—They don't know! Jos said, swinging Pascal around in a leggy swirl. Isn't it the damnedest, sweetest thing anybody's ever heard of?

—Do we, Pascal asked, have to tell them? That I'm thirteen, I mean?

—You're twelve, twerp, Jos said.

Holger signaled them in and sank into a chair to study the letter.

—I didn't say I was a professor, Pascal said, honest I didn't. I just sent the article, to see what they would say.

Holger leaned back in a robust fit of laughter.

—Rich, isn't it? Jos said, closing the door with a long push of his leg. Hug the scamp.

He lifted Pascal onto Holger's lap.

—Let's not tell anybody, Pascal said, until it's actually published, and even then I'll be revoltingly cool about it.

—Style, Jos said. Pascal and I are the only ones around this dump with real style.

—Franklin I'll tell, Pascal said, and that means Hugo and Mariana, too. Will you ask them not to tell, Holger?

—May I call you Holger, too? Jos asked. I'm not a prude and I don't blab. Professor Raskvinge!

34

Skipping and bouncing sideways, hands deep in his jeans pockets, Jos was saying to Meg and Rutger striding along with arms around each other's hips that he wished them a juicy tumble in the bracken. As for him, he had an hour's workout in the gym, a look at Anders's film now that some of it was spliced and edited, a half hour's posing for Tvemunding, and that if Meg would give him a kiss, friendly like, he would have the rest of the day by the balls. Meg without breaking stride hugged him in for a supple-tongued kiss which Jos secured for three long steps.

—Golly, she said, dancing her eyes.

—Slut, Rutger said.

—One more, Jos pleaded, trashing Rutger's hair. To give me a better excuse for the doltishly prolonged jacking off I've just added to my agenda.

Meg pushed her hands under his sweatshirt, playing a caress up his wide back and down to his lean hips.

—That's gross, Rutger said. Never mind that you're being studied by two nippers with big green eyes and their ears on backward. Hi, Franklin. Hi, Pascal. The embrace you're gawking at is purest theater. Or was. Quit that!

Meg, all innocence, dived at Rutger, tickled him in the ribs without mercy, and marched him off, blowing a kiss to Jos over her shoulder.

—Give yourself a fit, she said.

Jos spun on his heel, stomping.

—She ran her hand down inside your pants, Franklin said.

—With a raunchy squeeze, Jos sighed, his eyes closed. Wiggled her fingers on it, and then squeezed.

Pascal's Grundtvig Cap

Holger, climbing out of the gym pool, knocked water from first one ear and then the other, breathing through his mouth.

—What interested Montaigne, Hugo said, shaking water from his hair, was precision of emotion. The alert eye and attentive ear are cooperating with God and with the logic of creation.

—Precision of emotion, Holger said.

Figure and Ground

Franklin exchanged caps with Pascal, and Holger had better sense than to ask why.

— You know, Pascal said, you have an island, and in the island a lake, and in the lake an island.

— And, Franklin said, taking off his jacket, folding it, and laying it at his feet, in that island a pond, and in the pond an island.

Pascal took off his jacket, folded it, and laid it beside Franklin's.

— On the island in the pond is a spring making a pool, with a big rock in the pool, a frog sitting on it.

— A frog named McTaggart.

— What you're about to ask, Holger said, sitting, as their ramble around the park seemed to have become a milling about in one spot, with Franklin kneeling to untie a sneaker, is whether the earth is all an ocean with island continents, or is it all rock with ocean lakes?

— Yes, Franklin said, untying and prying off the other sneaker, but there are big lakes inside continents and big islands, like Greenland and England, in the oceans.

— The zebra problem, Holger said. And why are you unbuttoning your shirts?

— Who knows? Franklin said. I'm unbuttoning mine because Pascal's unbuttoning his.

— Correct distance, Pascal said. Talk about neat. Hugo says that the primitive mind is fussy about anything's being too far or too near, and that all our sense of distance is very old and basic. But what's neat is that primitive people and kids have the same sense of distance, correct distance I mean, and Mariana says it figures, as they're both cannibals. And then Hugo said correct distance is what civilization is all about, and that not having a sense of distance is feminine.

— There are two ways of doing this, Franklin said. Right now we can swap socks and shoes, and then shirts, until piece by piece we're in each other's clothes.

— While Hugo was talking, Mariana quietly tiptoed behind him and poured a glass of water over his head.

— Or we can skin ourselves to the knackers.

— Hugo didn't even flinch, water dripping from his chin and ears.

— That's from Lacan, Holger said, as well as from Lévi-Strauss. Women, as far as I know, have a more sensitive response to correct distance than men, in general, I would say.

Pascal, handing his shirt to Franklin, said that Hugo explained it wasn't a matter of gender but of male and female patterns amongst a bunch of people, like savages and kids.

—Oh well, Franklin said, oh. Hugo can explain everything except Hugo. It takes Mariana for that, but only when she's in her right mind.

Pascal's Blue Pinstripe Shirt

With white collar and glass buttons.

—Freedom from kinship, Hugo said, figures in all primitive ideas of paradise. A free choice of kinship, as in love or friendship, is a longing in us all. And this reshuffling of loyalties and attractions must be a finding, an invention. It's one of Yeshua's *logia*, also. Fate is, after all, a strategy.

Wolf Light

—Griddle the Witch was making a stew. Into it, for stock, she had put some kelp, some hoptoads, some cockroaches, several birdnests, some green scum from a pond, and bethought herself that a nasty juicy boy might be just the ingredient to round everything out.

—Me, probably, Franklin said, fluffing out his hair with his fingers.

—So, Mariana continued, she jumped onto her besom, taxied down the footlogs across the swamp, gave a neck-tickling cackle, and shot up into the middle air.

Pascal, Franklin knuckling his ribs, rolled backward and kicked over upright.

—What I want, Griddle said to herself, is a boy who has just stuffed himself with buttery hot cinnamon toast and drunk a mug of thick frothy hot chocolate, given him by his pretty big sister, who's fool enough to love him, and it would be even better if this nasty boy full of toast and chocolate had a friend just as nasty and just as full of toast and chocolate. They will stew up nice, those two.

—Door! Pascal said.

—Hugo, Franklin said, waffling the flat of his hand.

—Hugo and Holger, Mariana said.

—Britches, Pascal said. Where are my britches?

—Why? Franklin said. Holger'll blush anyway. Hugo won't notice.

—What a day, Hugo said, swiveling rain from the east, sleet from the west, wind straight down, with wild snow to make the mixture thoroughly idiotic. Spring, it calls itself. Here's Holger with me. What's going on here?

—Mud, Mariana said. Soccer practice got as far as mud from thatch to toes, and rats rolled up who turned out to be Pascal and Franklin under the muck, once I'd peeled them and stuck them in the shower. No dry clothes for Pascal, so they snuggled in the bedroll and had what they call a nap.

—Nap, Hugo said, giving Mariana a kiss. When Franklin looks that radiantly innocent, he has been diddling the system one way or another. Hello, Pascal.

—Hello, Hugo. Hello, Holger, Pascal said. Mariana made us stand side by side on a newspaper while she undressed us. Franklin said Jos would like it, so I liked it. Everything's different over here. Then she put us in the shower together.

—Here, Pascal, Franklin said, one of Hugo's T-shirts. Says Boy Scouts on it, and will come down to your knees. Fun. Me, I like

—Showing off, Mariana finished his sentence. And your dick and ballocks.

Hugo gave Franklin a kiss, and, to be fair, Pascal too.

—No favorites, he said.

—Thank you, Pascal said.

Tabletalk

There are no greater and lesser works of God. Creation is all one work, in a single style, from electron to star, we think, as a dog might suppose that the world extends from the orchard to the river.

Pascal's Undershirt

Narrow shoulder straps piped with a hairline of blue cunningly stitched.

Holger, his blue tent trig, its neat spare interior warm with congenial afternoon light under brailed flaps, pondered the moment, light as a function of time, the vibrant clarity of his pleasure in being alone in an expanse of wood and lake and sky, at peace with himself. The stillness was resonant and alive. Barefoot, he kept to his habitual decorum, however wildly unlikely it was that any other might intrude. By parachute? Pascal would ask.

No, that was Franklin.

Wildly unlikely, his own phrasing, was what Pascal would say. With an edged smile, he took off his jeans and the rakish briefs he'd bought because Hugo wore a pair like them, and Pascal had said with approval that everybody admired Hugo's racy underpants, and savored the freedom of his comfortably frayed and creased soft cotton shirt as his only garment. He felt both ascetic and immodest.

Sweet and crazy, Franklin would say.

Comfortable, Pascal.

But, my dear Icelandic Lutheran Reformed Evangelical Holger, he could hear Hugo saying with breezy candor, have the lucidity to see that you're emulating handsome Jos, who roves about the dorm in a ratty pullover, his Eagle Scout dick wigwagging as he treads.

A precise memory charged with redundant imagination:

Jos in Rutger and Anders's room arguing an assignment in trigonometry, his briefs rolled down in a ropy twist across his thighs, trifling fingers tugging his thickening penis as complacently as if petting a dog. Holger never entered a room, door open or closed, without knocking. Rutger's door was open.

—Don't mind Jos, Rutger said, our resident savage, probably noble.

—Whichwhat and since when? Jos said. Mind what?

And when Holger was back in his rooms, a smart rap on the door announced Jos, decent but with the bunt of his briefs strained forward.

—Honest, he said, I wasn't being cheeky just now. Awful to have to admit it, but I really wasn't aware I was monkeying with my dick. Anders says you'll think I was being impudent.

—Apology unnecessary, Jos. I should apologize to you for thinking it charming.

Jos, mouth opening little by little, gawked.

—You did? I know Tvemunding would, but he's crazy. You don't love me or anything like that, do you, hr. Sigurjonsson?

—Nope, Holger had said with grinning confidence, astonished that Jos's question had not upset him. What I find charming is my subjective prerogative, isn't it, and I thought you asked to call me Holger when you brought Pascal in to tell me his article was accepted?

—The secret article, Jos said. Oh yes, well, Holger then.

—I like that.

—We're talking crisscross, I think, Sir. I mean, Holger. It wouldn't bother me in the least if you loved me. I'm broad-minded that way.

—You're a good boy, Jos.

—And charming. By subjective prerogative. I've got to know what that means.

—Subjective, in the privacy of my mind. Prerogative, that what I think is my own business. Our apologies are symmetrical: both for a disrespect.

—Where's the disrespect in my subjective prerogative charm? Love those words!

—You're supposed to resent it, I think.

—Not me! Who says?

—Something called the world.

—The world can stuff it.

A double rap on the door: Pascal spinning in on his heel.

—Oh wow! he said. Big Jos, and in his nappies.

—Hi, squirt, Jos said.

Pascal's Britches

—Iceland, Pascal said, is a nest of volcanoes, like the Galapagos Islands. The bases of the volcanoes flowed together, like chocolate sauce in a banana split, to make a plateau. In Iceland the plateau is above, the Galapagos, below sea level. Where you have meadows and sheep and Lutherans in Iceland, you have the ocean between hilltops in the Galapagos, that is, between islands.

After a victory celebration of banana splits with Holger and Jos, Pascal chose as more reward to spend the night with Franklin, at Hugo's. But, Pascal insisted, not to tell about the article's acceptance, for which he would choose his own good time. Jos agreed.

—A good secret is something sweet up the sleeve.

Franklin met them at the door wearing a gray sweatshirt and white gym socks, otherwise naked, his lizardy stipe of a penis poking straight out over a roundly solid scrotum.

—Hi, Holger, he said. Hi, Pascal.

—The ingenuous state of nature in which Franklin greets you, Hugo said, was devised by its exemplar soon after you called.

While Holger made his devoirs to Mariana, who was sewing buttons on shirts, and to Hugo, who was writing in a bound notebook with gridded pages, Pascal with studied unconcern doffed first his short pants and briefs, which he folded pedantically as he talked about the subglacial and undersea lavas of Iceland, and placed with Franklin's clothes in an oblong wicker basket, and then sat to untie his shoes. Franklin helped.

Above the basket, on a shelf, was a triangular Cub Scout neckerchief, its blue border punctuated with chevrons, wolf face, and *fleur de lys* in a square, a blue beanie, the German magazine *Philius*, an aluminum canteen in a canvas jacket, with strap. Above the shelf, Hugo's painting of Tom Agernkop.

—Nested order, Holger said.

—I'll buy the nested part, Mariana remarked, biting thread.

Pascal, pulling on a T-shirt, said:

—I don't go around the dorm like this. Exactly the opposite, interestingly enough. This is my and Franklin's uniform over here.

—Who's your roommate at the dorm? Mariana asked.

—I'm the only Grundtvigger, Pascal said, with a room to myself.

—Because, Holger explained, by age he's lower school, but academically upper.

—And if, Hugo said archly, somebody who's presently inspecting his virile member as if he'd never seen it before and is wondering what it's for, gets his grade average up, not your v.m. but your grades, he can move in with Pascal, and Mariana and I won't hear mouse squeaks, squishy slurps, and puppy yelps half the night.

—You've scandalized Holger, Mariana said, and he's leaving.

—Can't be away any longer from the dorm, Holger said. Jos is in charge, but his authority runs thin.

—Wait! Pascal said, turning Holger around to hug him.

A whisper from Mariana, and Franklin scrambled up from the floor and added his hug.

Hugo walked Holger back to the dorm, talking about Aramaic phrasing discernible in New Testament Greek.

Pascal's Underpants

Delay of iodine in kelp, rondure of acorn, fit of cup, flex of mouse, nod of helve, tilted pileus mushroom warp, tangle of floss, musk of straw, dent of cowrie, attar of olives, nubby scammony nuchal pink warm under spun cotton knit fine.

43

Jos in a dingy workout shirt foxy with sweat and parting at the shoulders, slim jeans, and scruffy sneakers, asked Holger in the hallway, between classes, if he could have a quick word with him, please.

—I need, he said, to cut German and English, which I'm up on and fluent in, anyway, and gym, which Hugo will have my butt for, though I work out more than anybody in this dump. I got through chemistry, but I'd like to catch some sleep. Would it be too much to ask if I could sack out on your floor for an hour or two?

—If you need to, Holger said. You aren't into narcotics, are you, Jos?

—Oh Lord, no! Jos said.

—The apartment's been cleaned for the day, Holger said, shutting the door. Nobody will bother you. Insomnia?

—Well, no, Jos said. Night before last, we won't go into that, I skipped lots of sleep, and didn't sleep at all last night, and it has caught up with me. If I could stretch out on the carpet here, with maybe that thingummy across the back of that chair for a pillow?

—You'll be more comfortable in bed, Holger said. Clean sheets, even.

—You're a brick, Jos said, undoing the brass buttons of his jeans. Fact is, he added with a rueful look, I jacked off all fucking night. Decidedly retarded, and not recommended by the Boy Scout handbook, but there we are. Sorry, no underbritches.

—Lend you pyjamas, Holger said.

—Mna. Maybe a top? This sweatshirt smells like the zoo.

Max Bill

Horizontal blue, diagonal red, vertical green.

45

—In the bedroom, Holger said to Pascal when he twirled in, we have Jos, who said he was dead for sleep, and whom I've let snooze through dinner.

—Crazy, Pascal said. Jos in your sack. So we start bed check here.

—Let's see, Holger said, if he isn't ready to get up. We can make him a snack.

One arm over his head, the other out straight, Jos, smiling awake, peeped at Holger and Pascal from narrow eyelids.

—Where am I? he asked. What time is it, and who am I?

— A long boy name of Jos, Holger said, with a pair of handsome eyes, feathery eyelashes, and wrecked hair. The rest of him is rather operatically twisted into the covers.

—And, Jos said, is this The Buttermilk Elf?

—Hello, Jos, Pascal said. You're wearing Holger's jammies.

—Only the top, Jos said, kicking loose from sheet and eiderdown, swiveling out of bed to stand on his toes, stretch, and yawn.

—Like a lion, Pascal said.

—Be nice to me, friend Pascal, as nice as Holger's been. I'm feeling sort of unreal and discontinuous.

—Scramble you some eggs? Holger asked. Toast, marmalade, a sausage or two? You've dreamed right through dinner, where your absence was commented on, imaginatively.

—I'll have some of the marmalade and toast, too, Pascal said. I know where everything is, and can do the eggs. You run them around in the pan with a fork, right? Lots of butter. Is there a spring in your dick, Jos, that makes it bounce like that when you walk?

—Somebody, Jos said, is not as undescended of balls as he used to be, and probably has high-octane hormones squishing around inside him, wouldn't you say, hr. Sigurjonsson? Holger, I mean. Feels good, doesn't it, Grasshopper? Was it getting taken for a senior academician with beard and dandruff, one soon to be published in a magazine big as a phonebook, that made the sap rise from your pink toes, upward, and upward?

Pascal danced a tricky step, grinning and snapping his fingers.

—I like you to kid me, Jos. It gives you such pleasure.

—Easy on the salt, Pascal, Holger said.

—Why, Pascal asked, did you sack out here all afternoon, as long as we're being personal?

—Because, Mushrump, I didn't sleep for two nights in a row, one given generously to guarding Rutger and Meg while they did it more or less all night, whimpering and sighing with approval of each other's anatomy, that's quite a story, and then last night I practiced self-abuse, as they say, from beddy-bye until I heard birds twittering. Thought my mind had gone, but they were real birds, and it was daylight, and my bold fellow here, who, yes, does have a spring inside to make him waggle like this, was still ranting to make a baby. Nature's awful, you know. No regard for decency or model behavior.

—Whether we're to believe this, Holger said, is up to us, isn't it, Pascal?

—I'm jealous, Pascal said. I can say that, can't I, Holger?

—Ha, Jos said, you have a room all to yourself. Asgar slept through it all, but woke up, all eyes, for the last gusher, which was as sweet as deep up a girl, and called me a pervert and a maniac. Not, you understand, for jacking off, as he was careful to explain, but for when I was jacking off, before breakfast. You did good with those scrumpled eggs, Professor Raskvinge, and is there more milk?

Studio

Jos's eyes, lakeblue discs in eyelashes like the outline of an elmleaf drawn with a drenched Chinese brush, stared in so short a focus at Holger's they seemed slightly crossed.

—Do I really look like that?

—It's a splendid likeness, Holger said. Yes, you look like that.

—It's still only a study, Hugo said. Can't call it a painting when it's just Jos with his wrists crossed on top of his head, weight on both feet.

—And my eyes look like that?
—Yes, Hugo said.

47
—What Iceland has that's really wild, Pascal said, is volcanoes erupting under glaciers.
—Crazy, Franklin said.
—Blows hunks of glacier into the air, melts the glacier, boils the glacier into steam. Drowns Lutherans for kilometers around.

The Present Is Another Country
—Well, Jos said, so he does have bits of eggshell still sticking to his curls. That's all the niftier.

Holger had walked Pascal to Hugo and Mariana's after bed check, had visited awhile, and on his return to his rooms found Jos sitting against the door, knees up, cricket cap on backward, in his low-waisted sweatpants, lumpy white socks, and gymnast's tank top.

—Can I come in? he said, sliding his hand from inside his pants, tying the drawstring, and getting up with a nimble bounce.

—Absolutely, Holger said. I was just seeing Pascal over to spend the night with Franklin Landarbejder. One of our modern improvements on the past. They snuggle, I suppose, in a sleeping bag.

—Over where Franklin's clothes are, in the wicker basket, Jos said, and his scouting gear, next to me in paint on Hugo's easel, and with Hugo and Mariana making the bed creak and jiggle.

Holger shrugged.

—Cocoa, milk? Even beer, which I'm not supposed to offer you.

—I won't snitch, Jos said. I need to talk a bit. Pascal would want me to have a beer, the sweet little nipper.

—In which case, Holger said, we'll follow Pascal's wishes.

—What I want to talk about is sort of raunchy, so I might as well throw in, to see how you're going to take this, that I think you and Pascal being pals is a good thing.

—Am I supposed to know, Holger asked, what you're talking about, Jos?

—Well, Jos said, so he does have bits of eggshell still sticking to his curls. That's all the niftier.

—My question remains the same.

—OK, Jos said, smiling amiably and sitting on the floor, knees up, his back against a chair occupied by books, new botanical and geographical journals, a rolled map, a soccer jersey, and a musette bag.

—Let me clear the chair for you, Holger said. You don't have to sit on the floor.

—Prefer it, Jos said. Good beer. And you're a good man.

Holger sat in his leather reading chair across from him, having shuttered the venetian blinds, replacing his shoes with bedroom slippers.

—I'll blurt it all out, Jos said. I don't know, maybe you can tell me why I want you to know all this, but I do. A kind of sharing, as you'll see. It's nothing scary, and not a problem. About two weeks back I fucked Meg. Not *made love to* or *slept with*, those stupid words, but fucked. That is, Rutger and I fucked Meg. He's fucked her just about every day since he's been here, and they'd been doing it well before, wholly into each other.

—As the whole school knows, Holger said, with the possible exception of the Master and fru Eglund, McTaggart, and the kitchen cat.

—Well, Jos said, I've never been what you would call buddies with Rutger, as friendships go, though we've gotten lots closer this term, and I've sort of fallen in with him and Meg together. Three friends are different from two friends, you know? Why the smile?

—Thinking of something else, Holger said. Go on.

—Got to piss. Your bathroom's down the hall, isn't it?

—On the left.

—Your rooms are like a comfortable house, Jos said over his loud midbowl stream. It's good to get away from my Spartan jail cell. I'll leave in a bit, huh?

—It's early, Holger said. I've nothing I have to do before bedtime. Your beer's where you were sitting.

When Jos came back to the sitting room his sweatpants were rolled into a wad which he tossed onto the chair.

—Very becoming, Holger said, undershirt and socks.

—Wasn't wearing briefs. You don't mind? You come and watch Hugo paint me in Fanny fuck all, though my weewee is in its hang position there. It has, however, come within a hair of standing straight up. There was the afternoon Mariana came in with groceries, and kept saying how handsome I am. It gave a jump, and nodded, which she saw, and let me know with a sweet wink. Which made him jump again. And I keep having the feeling that Hugo, if I gave him a little encouragement, would haul me on his shoulder over to the bed and love me until we both passed out. Holger, what are those two books over there, *Growth and Form?*

—D'Arcy Thompson, a British scholar, on the laws governing natural structures. It's a book to know. Pascal has read it twice, I believe, and it's one of our favorite books to talk about.

Jos took the books down and opened them in the pool of lamplight on the carpet by Holger's chair.

—Do you know R. Buckminster Fuller's work? Holger asked.

—Geodesic buildings, Jos said. Sticks held in suspension by wires. A new kind of solid geometry. And a world map in triangles. Pascal has one on his wall.

—And Klee's notebooks? Holger asked.

—No. You have them here?

Holger fetched them, and sat with Jos on the floor.

—The Botany Club, he said, is going to start a project in which I take them through Leonardo, Fibonacci, and Klee.

Jos pointed to the framed Klee on the wall.

—Hugo and Mariana admired that the evening of the battle Adam and Franklin had down the corridor. They took it, I'm afraid, as evidence of my appreciation of the fine arts, but it's there for its accuracy of botanical forms.

—Show me, Jos said.

The Blind Folksinger

A steady clatter of rain on the skylight accompanied a Bach partita on Hugo's phonograph.

—Earliest memories, Hugo said, are problematic. They can be constructed from later information, from family folklore.

—Not this, Holger said. What I remember is a sunny room, vivid colors as of cloth, greens and blues, and a window brilliant with the light of an Icelandic spring. In this scene I am in a woman's lap, perhaps my nurse, perhaps my mother. I had just been bathed. The oval porcelain tub is nearby. A clean fluffy towel and the odor of talcum are part of the memory. And this woman played with my penis, bouncing it with the flat of her hand. It is a very happy memory, you understand.

—Was she, Hugo asked, perhaps only drying under the foreskin, which can be a tight fit in a baby, and you were enjoying it?

—The odd thing is that I see this memory as if I were a third person, looking on, yet enjoying the pleasure of having my penis fondled.

—You're remembering a mirror, Hugo said. A woman would sit with a charming baby so that she could see herself in a bedroom mirror. Our culture has conditioned us to dwell on the image of a happy mother and winsome infant. How old were you?

—Not more than two, as I figure.

—Does this come in a dream?

—No. It's a waking memory, but it visits regularly, as in Proust. Shaving, bathing, or in a sunny room.

—The psychological weather.

—Yes. But what I've got up the courage to narrate is not this, but an event much later, when I was ten or eleven. Saturday is always a fateful day, and this was a Saturday. I remember the clothes I was wearing, because they were new, bought for the beginning of the school term: a blue wool sweater. I was vain of the fit, and of its quality. It was of heavy wool, with flecks of red and gray in its strong Icelandic blue. And I had new long corduroy trousers, which swished. And all of this finery fitted in with an outing my favorite uncle had arranged. We drove into the country, to see a man my uncle had met years before, and wanted to see again. My uncle was a schoolteacher and keen on Icelandic folkways, legends and ballads, that sort of thing. A ride in an automobile was exciting enough, over country roads, but to be going to a farm was even more exciting. But I mustn't draw this out.

—As you will, Holger. But I gather this is for my ears only, and Mariana will be along, and Franklin with his double.

—The essentials, then, and we can deal with the implications in good time. The blind folksinger my uncle wanted me to meet, and hear, lived with his sister and her husband on a farm about as remote as you can get. Dingy sheep with black legs, ponies, green hills all around. A very old white stone house, with barns and pens and sties also of stone. Dogs barked us in for half a kilometer, and I remember rings of hawks in a cloudy sky. The people were simple country folk but with those deep traditions which contain respect for scholarship and a familiarity with the Bible. There was a radio, I remember, which picked up Reykjavik. The interior was purest Ibsen, reeking of the past. Why are you smiling?
—Because I'm enjoying the tale.
—I don't see how you could be. The Bach partita helps. Well, country people, a blind folksinger. I'd never met a blind person, but I understood, before we left, how he lived in a world of familiar surfaces and spaces, and how his ears served as his eyes. He sang, accompanying himself on just such a harmonium as you and Mariana have, which you've taught Franklin and Pascal to sing so prettily to. I remember some lines of a spooky ballad, sung in a high, keen, perhaps falsetto voice.
—Countertenor, Hugo said.
—Yes, countertenor. The lines were:

Long is one night,
But longer are two,
O how can I wait for three?

When, later in life, I saw a photograph of Walt Whitman, I realized that they could have been taken for twins, right down to the shape of beard and hair. The faces, especially the eyes, were the same, strange as it is that blind and seeing eyes should resemble each other. He made his sister describe me to him, and I must have blushed wildly to hear myself itemized and assessed. Red-brown hair, sweet eyes, freckles, the handsome blue sweater, which the folksinger asked to feel, the new corduroy trousers, whose sound he'd wondered about. He ran his fingers over my face, and held my hands in his for an uncomfortably long time.

The phone rang. Hugo said into it:

—Lovely. Holger's here. He's telling me about his childhood. Oh yes. We'll have a fire, against the damp.

And to Holger:

—Mariana. She'll be along in a bit. Says hello.

—Well, then, to get to the substance of all this. There came a moment when Uncle and the sister were searching out old hymnals and some kind of folklore journal, these being in long chests painted over with trolls and floral swirls, and the folksinger enticed me over and whispered that he would like me to walk him to the outhouse. It didn't occur to me until later that he would have known the way perfectly, but I felt a measure of virtue in leading the blind to a call of nature. He kept his hand on my shoulder all the way. I won't try to describe the outhouse, a new experience for me. Once inside, he asked if anybody were near, and when I said no, he said that I should make water first, his words, make water. I did, feeling very sure of myself as a child of the city among such countrified and primitive people. My new togs enforced my sense of superiority, as the speech of these farm people was as antique as their strange clothes from the century before. The blind folksinger's trousers came up to his chest, and his shirt had pleats and a frill of lace at the collar, and his coat had the biggest buttons I'd ever seen. And then, when I was about to tuck in and zip up, the old codger fumbled for my penis, and got it. I'd never felt a hand other than my own on that tender organ, and I was mystified, scared, and obliging all at once. I won't try to analyze my emotions, except to say that my fear gave way to pleasure, and to the sweetness of stolen pleasure, at that. I want to be very truthful, Hugo, because I think this is a key to something that will probably be obvious to you, but which as yet isn't to me.

—We'll see, Hugo said. This gets better and better.

—He was an astute old cooter, and said we musn't dally in the outhouse, even though my little man, as he called it, was springy stiff and feeling wonderfully sexy. His age, by the way, was probably late thirties or early forties, that is, an old man to my few years. So I zipped up, with my erection making a bump in my new corduroys, and as we walked back he sang some lilting ballad with a jolly refrain. He held me hard by the shoulder. When we got back to the house, he went no farther than the door, through which he said in a loud voice that the young gentleman wanted to see the black-faced sheep in the upper pasture. Where we walked, and when he asked if we were out of sight of the house, or of anybody, he mastered, by touch, the working of my zipper, while I stood in a kind of trance. He kept asking, in the kindest of voices, if I liked what he was doing, and I answered, quite truthfully, *yes*. He wanted to know if I did what he was doing by myself, and I remember how wonderfully wicked I felt when I replied that I did. But when he wanted to know if I had friends who did what he was doing, I said no, and he said that I must get new friends who would. He made me promise that, that very night, when I was home, I would play with myself, as he called it. We walked farther into the pastures, with sheep and cows staring at us. On top of a knoll I realized that we were walking in a great circle around the farm. And I must tell that not long after he'd jacked me off, he asked if I would like it again, and I eagerly unzipped for a replay. This time we did it together, his hand over mine, and he kissed me on my head as I reported on my rising pleasure.

—Good God, Holger! Hugo said. You were initiated into the boyish mysteries by a wizard of the *huldufolk*. Your cock's probably magic. I don't dare tell Mariana.

—You're the only person I've ever told this, you understand. At the time, it was not something I could tell anybody. It was, indeed, a rite of passage. That afternoon ended with the folksinger saying that I was not a boy but an angel, with everyone pleased that I had brought joy to the house for a few hours, and there was a long ballad before we left, which interested my uncle, as he'd never heard it, and asked to return to take it, and others, down. So there you have it, friend Hugo: a kind of primal event, as clear as I can tell it.

—Did you return?

—Yes, several times, and with similar ruses for being out of sight long enough for our stolen pleasure. And I was faithful to his injunction. That was a lovely secret that I hoarded: an adult who wanted me to feel sexual pleasure.

—He didn't take you in his mouth?

—Well, yes, he did. I was trying to spare you that.

—I can't think why. And the real question is why you wanted me to know this rustic tale from wildest Iceland.

—Isn't it the Freudian *es* of the formula? Where it was, there must I come to be.

—I couldn't possibly say. Holger, old boy, I know exactly nothing of your emotional life.

—There isn't any. I was engaged for a while when I was at the university, but broke it off when in a dismal revelation all I could see was a prospect of gin, bridge, and television. Moreover, she was Catholic, with transparent designs for my conversion. And smoked.

—You should be cheerful the rest of your life for so narrow an escape. No wonder you love to hie off on weekends to the darkest forests. As for your psychological backtracking, I see more in the earlier memory. It's a painting by Mary Cassatt. Only thing in my past I can put beside it is the day I showed the postman my dick. Everybody in Kindergarten had liked seeing it, and I was sure he would, too.

Byggvir the Barley

The light that had been so radiantly pellucid all afternoon took on bronze tones in the pinewood. On the slow rise of a slope soft with a flooring of pine needles Holger, Pascal, and Jos laid out provender.

—A good ten kilometers, Jos said.

—I've never walked so far, Pascal said. Not all at a go, anyway.

—A long walk is one of my ways of keeping body and soul on speaking terms, Holger said.

—Neatest of ideas, Jos said, to take the bus to Tidselby and walk back to Grundtvig. You didn't think I'd come along, did you, Holger? Couldn't say no to Pascal, though I did come and ask if you really wanted me. I mean, it's your walk, with Pascal. Deviled eggs! Chocolate squares!

—Catered, Holger said. Fru Vinterberg, for a modest fee, composed this feed: sandwiches, buttermilk, coffee, deviled eggs, cheese, no end to it. Paper napkins, even. And gave her motherly blessing to a picnic in the country.

—Didn't comment, did she, Jos asked with his mouth full of sandwich, on how you spoil Pascal rotten?

—Jos, Holger said to Pascal, pointedly, is a horrible example of the kind of person who knows no ground between a very correct formal politeness and unbuttoned familiarity. The old Jos used to be a model Danish schoolboy to his housemaster, and the new Jos treats him as the sailor next bunk over in the forecastle of a herring trawler.

—So? Jos asked. We've sat up all night talking about a hundred things, and I've slept off a carnal binge in your bed, and you like to see me being drawn and painted by crazy Hugo.

—It's a good picture, Pascal said. Are those pickles in that paper boat? He's going to paint me, too, skinny as I am, and Franklin, but maybe with clothes, or some clothes, on. He's done Franklin nude several times.

—Is he a good painter, Holger? Jos asked. I think he is.

—He says, Pascal answered, that painting is his way of showing others what he sees. If he were a poet or a writer, he could say what he sees. Franklin and I asked why he didn't just photograph things, and he said he might, at that. But wouldn't quit painting. There are lots of sketchbooks all of Mariana.

—It is my opinion, probably worthless, Jos said, that everything Hugo does is sex, one way or another.

—Talk about seeing yourself in others, Holger said.

Pascal grinned around a deviled egg.

—If I weren't me, I'd like to be Hugo, Jos said. I don't know about looking after all those scouts, or teaching Sunday School, but I'd like to do the brainy things he does with the big dictionaries and books, and paint, and bounce Mariana four or five times a day, and maybe even love on Franklin. Does he do that, Pascal, love on Franklin?

—Do you think I know, Jos? Pascal asked, putting a foot against his knee and pushing.

—Boys, Holger said.

—Probably does, Jos said. Is there any more buttermilk?

—Finish mine, Holger said. I'm ready for chocolate squares and coffee. After which, I think these soft pine needles, so lovely warm and crunchy, want me to stretch out on them and have a lazy rest, good for the digestion.

—Holger's ideas are unfailingly top-notch, Jos said. First, a wild bus to Tidselby, with its sights, cabbage patches on the high street, and a row of piglets having lunch on fru Pig. Secondly, a nifty hike, very comradely, and with news of the flora and fauna along the way. If Pascal is as educated at twelve as Holger is at twenty-whatever, what in the name of sweet Jesus will Pascal sound like when he's Holger's decrepit age? Thirdly, a picnic in the woods. And now pallet drill on sunny pine needles. May I be totally comfortable, Holger?

—What now, scamp?

—Discard my pants? Which are Asgar's anyway, and are biting my hipbones. Mine, with the slit pockets, were too nasty for an outing among moral Danes. Shirt off will feel good, too.

—Dapper undergear, Holger said.

Jos, brown and smiling in a jockstrap with a finely meshed net pouch, tapped his broad and thick pectorals with admiring fingers, the knobby furrows of his ribs, the grooved plane of his long abdomen.

—You're beautiful, Jos, Pascal said. An ancient Greek.

—Work hard enough at it, Jos said. High-tech tough, the supporter. The fit is perfect, as the waist and cinches latch together with Velcro facings, the cup too. See?

—So you assemble it on your person?

—And rip it off, Jos said. Infant friend Pascal, if you'll lie on that side of sleepy Holger, at right angles, like, I'll lie on this side, using him for a companionable pillow, all of us wickedly close.

—Feels naughty, Pascal said.

—Friendly, Jos said.

—Slit pockets, Pascal said.

—I knew that hadn't slipped past Pascal, Holger said.

—For making my dick happy in class. Ankle on knee, book propped just so, and one can frig away fifty minutes which otherwise would be the dullest in northwest Europe. Tom and I sit beside each other in five classes, and inspire and encourage each other. Should Pascal hear this, Holger?

—Nerd! Pascal said.

—Should *I* hear it? Holger asked, running fingers into Jos's hair, and into Pascal's.

—Holger can hear it, Jos said, if he won't snitch to housemaster Sigurjonsson.

—Which of those two is being lain on by two Grundtviggers in the sun, deliciously warm?

—Holger, Pascal said. Housemaster Sigurjonsson won't exist again until we're back. Masturbation was invented by the god Hermes.

—Jesus, Jos said.

—Hugo told me that, Pascal said. Me and Franklin.

—He's the one who delivers telegrams from Olympus, isn't he? Jos asked. Wears a derby with wings, and has cute little wings on his ankles, and clears his way with two snakes fucking on a stick? Otherwise dressed for a bath?

—That's him, Pascal said.

—Is it still Holger, Jos asked, who's messing with my hair?

—Still Holger, Holger said.

—Thing is, Jos went on, is not to mind if you come, and to brazen out looking as if you've broken an egg in your pants. Tom, the god Hermes of NFS Grundtvig, worked out the technique. No underwear, old pants with the pockets scissored out, and the degree of covert operation required. In McTaggart's world's dullest classes, you can unzip and jack away in the open, behind the big English anthology. Latin and Ethics, inside, and stay on one's guard. Geometry's a ticklish business also, with caution and vigilance repaid, especially as Walliser is some species of religious fanatic. But Art Appreciation is a snap, what with the room darkened for slides.

—How, Pascal asked, can you pay attention?

—What, Cricket, do you think about when you whack off?

—Nothing, Pascal said.

—Holger still with us? Jos asked, rolling his head under Holger's fingers.

—Still here, but barely.

—Sigurjonsson not likely to come back suddenly? Paying attention's no problem. I pay better attention in Art Appreciation and Geometry for having my dick feel like the last movement of Beethoven's Ninth. In Ethics and English I'm making up for the scarcity of spirit in Bakke and McTaggart. Tom, what a champion, can come while sight-reading Latin.

—The tenacious diligence of it all is what gets through to me, Holger said. The biology is plain enough.

Pascal reached back and laced fingers with Holger.

—For all our whiffling our peters as a pair, Jos said, like before Latin when we're good at happening on each other in my room or his, to work tone into our members, you know, and breeze, he's never made a pass at me, loyal to gawky Lemuel all the way. Who, Lemuel I mean, is of a reticence, circumspect, except, natch, with Tom. Lacks imagination, Lemuel.

—Are you being depraved by all this, Pascal? Holger said. I am.

—If I am, is it OK?

—Why not? Jos said, rolling over and propping his chin on Pascal's forehead. Pascal has lots of rascal in him.

—Franklin, my buddy, Pascal said, found the rascal, and likes him. He's a nice rascal. I can talk Jos Sommerfeld, too.

—And, Holger said, Pascal's finding the brainy boy in Franklin.

Jos rolled back over, resting his head on Holger's abdomen.

—Not being too familiar, am I? he asked with an indicative bobble.

—You're an affectionate person, Jos, Holger said.

—Shameless, Jos said.

—But with style, Holger said. Much would have to be forgiven you, except for style, shouldn't we say in all candor?

—Housemaster Sigurjonsson has returned, Pascal said.

—Mna, Jos said, rising to hands and knees, he's taking the afternoon off.

He crossed Holger on all fours, stood and rolled his shoulders, cupped a hand over the pouch of his jockstrap, appraising its swell, clucked through puckered lips, prodded Pascal's shoulder lightly with his toe, and sat beside him, shoving a hand with walking fingers under his shirt.

—Talk about being familiar, Pascal said.

—Nobody's looking, Jos said.

—Somebody's untying my shoes, Pascal said. And winkling off my socks.

—Holger's still here, Holger said, but how much longer I can't promise.

—That's my zipper!

—Squeaky clean didies, Jos said, extra small. Shake him out of his shirt, Holger, while I deprive you of your shoes. We're all, before hr. Sigurjonsson comes home, going to have a big rough threeway hug, just as God made us, because the world is full of hopeless nerds afraid of being touched and too fucking mean to cuddle a puppy, and we're sweet daffy friends, yes? Oh yes!

—Oh wow! Pascal said.

—Undo Holger in various places, Jos said, and skin him to the balls. He's more or less covered with red hair all over, which will tickle.

Holger, crimson, nevertheless stood for Pascal to unbutton his shirt with awkward fingers. He unbuckled his belt himself, and had begun on the brass buttons of his hiking shorts when Jos took over, deftly, and hauled down shorts and briefs together.

—Jimbang goofy! Pascal said, Jos lifting him into Holger's arms.

—That's the spirit, Jos said, collapsing them onto the pine needles with a robust, pulling hug. Pascal between them, Holger and Jos, hands locked in the small of each other's backs, rocked into momentum enough to roll over twice.

—They lay still. Jos, caressing Holger's back, nuzzled his face in Pascal's hair. He kissed the back of Pascal's neck, relinquishing the doubleness of his embrace to hug Pascal alone.

—Your turn, he said, rolling away.

Pascal wrapped arms and legs around Holger.

—That's the style, Cricket, Jos said. Nothing shy. I'm right here, greedy, when you've squeezed Holger breathless.

—OK, Pascal said, tousled of hair, dazed and vague of eye, but you and Holger have to hug, too, next.

They complied, laughing happily, Jos drumming his heels on the ground.

—We're stuck all over with pine needles, Jos said, sitting up and gasping. One on my dick. Tell you what: I started this, and I see how to wrap it up before hr. Sigurjonsson puts a stop to it. I get one more warm and wild hug from Pascal, and Holger gets one, exactly as warm and wild, and then we turn back into stodgy Danes out hiking, huh?

Warm and wild hugs hugged, Holger brushed and picked pine needles off Pascal with a dreamy gentleness, and held his underpants for him to step into, and settled their fit.

—You're going to dress me?

His question was quiet, matter of fact.

—Mind?

—What is there to mind?

Pascal ran his arms into the sleeves of his shirt, and looked pleased and proud as Holger buttoned it on. Hiking pants, socks, shoes, followed.

—I can tie my shoes, at least.

—No, Holger said, I tie them.

—Friendly, Jos said. I'm loving this. My Christian feast of neighborliness worked, you see.

51

The next Ice Age began in the fourteenth century. Cold wet winters advanced the prows of the glaciers. Harvests in the north of Europe failed year after year, until the vineyards of England were abandoned. In Scandinavia and Iceland wheat and barley farmers became fishermen. Art became speculative and ironic.

Lions Have No Historians

He drank only well water, the blind folksinger, never spirits. Is your hair coppery gold, he had asked, or is it the white of meal, as with the old stock? He believed in the hidden folk. I know too much about them to doubt that they are. They are, you know, he had said, with a squeeze for Holger's shoulder. They are wise. Your smallclothes are cunningly sewn, he had said, and your hands are as soft as a girl's. The hidden folk sent you to me, and the debt I owe them is large.

53

—Holger! Jos said, coming in without knocking, what the fuck happened?

—Sprained my ankle, Holger said. In the gym.

—Lemuel said you'd met Biology on crutches. Here I am. What can I do? Where's Pascal?

Holger was in his easy chair, his bandaged foot on a stool.

—The horse, Holger said. I was getting good at it, and next thing I knew I'd come a cropper, with a shooting pain in the ankle. Hobbled over to the infirmary, where Matron tied on twenty or so meters of gauze, as you see, issued me crutches, and commanded me to stay off my foot for three or four days.

—Awesome, Jos said. And not like you. You're as unbreakable and permanently healthy as crazy Hugo.

—Jos, Holger said, the front of your pants, which look as if they have been worn in a ship's galley by six generations of teenaged apprentice cooks, is sopping wet.

—Don't change the subject. I want to know what I can do to help. I'll move in, bring you things, pour and stir your medicine. Didn't you get any medicine?

—Aspirin.

—Two loads, Jos said of his pants. Came in English and in Ethics. I didn't take time to change. Apologies, if needed.

—Of course not. See who's at the door.

It was Mariana.

—Holger, poor baby! she said. Hi, Jos. Holger, Hugo called and said you'd fallen ass over heels doing gymnastics but that you hadn't broken anything, only wrenched a tendon in your ankle. What did Matron, the bitch, do for you?

—Bound it up. Says I'm to stay off it.

—Didn't put anything on it?

—Nope.

—Not even Baume Bengué? I suspected as much, which is why I'm here, on my lunch hour, with the goods.

She took from her purse a large bottle.

—The liniment of Sloan. It's really just turpentine and red peppers. Comes from Pastor Tvemunding, who swears by it. What's more, it works. I daub it on Hugo all the time. It did wonders for an ankle I sprained last year. Got any cotton swabs?

—In the bathroom cabinet, Jos.

—Also, Jos, put on a kettle, Mariana said. Have you peed your pants? Bring a washcloth, a basin for the hot water, and I'll unwind this silly bandage.

—I'm not used to all this attention, Holger said. Florence Nightingale and Jos. I wouldn't ask about his pants again, if I were you.

—Oh come on, Holger, she said, busily unwrapping gauze from his foot, I wasn't born yesterday. Does it hurt?

—Throbs.

—Kettle's on, Jos said. Basin and washcloth here, plus a sack of cotton balls. In which drawer are your briefs, Holger?

—Top left.

—I see your gym shorts on the bed, if I may borrow them, and a pair of underbritches, and then frøken Landarbejder will be spared my depraved pants.

—With bottomless pockets, Mariana said sweetly. I do happen to be Franklin's big sister.

One Hundred Staring Sheep

Long slopes of bluebells and buttercups under windy running clouds. The ranny mouse, the blind folksinger said, let us free the ranny mouse from his sweet nest in the bag of your smallclothes, that smell so clean and are of such soft fabric, so neatly sewn. What a nice sleeping mouse he is, and grows so fast when he wakes.

55

—Couldn't get here before now, Pascal said, and have rather disgraced myself, at that. I heard you'd been to class on crutches, and then that Hugo was taking your geography class, and I asked McTaggart to be excused from English, as I'd heard you'd had an accident, and McTaggart asked what that had to do with anything, least of all cutting his class. And when I said you might need me, he laughed, and I already had my foot back to kick him when I was smart enough to see that kicking the English master, as he deserved, wasn't a bright idea, so I had to stay, but Hugo, of course, excused me from gym without my even asking. Go look after Holger, he said.

—He sent Mariana at noon, Holger said. The odor of turps pervading the room is Sloan's Liniment, as per the bottle of it there, which Mariana and Jos dabbed on my foot, which is only sprained, after soaking it in boiling water. Cooked it, I think.

—Jos?

—He was here first, after I hobbled from the infirmary. Mariana, who has a degree in nursing children, you know, was incensed at Matron's treatment, and did it all over, her way, or, rather, Pastor Tvemunding's way. Sloan's Liniment is Capsicum oleoresin, methyl salicylate, oil of camphor, pine oil, and turpentine.

—Mexican red peppers in urinal cleaner, Pascal said. Oh wow.

—What about some tea and toast with marmalade, friend Pascal? I'm to stay off my foot. I've been hoping you'd turn up.

—Don't dare get up. I know where everything is.

Halfway down the hall, he turned and ran back to give Holger a hug and nuzzled kiss, getting hugged in return.

—Cups, saucers, plates, Pascal said after an interval of putting the kettle on and buttering bread for the oven, cream and sugar, spoons and knives. Let's move the coffee table here. I can sit on the floor. Holger, are those Jos's pants over the foot of your bed?

—Sodden with sperm? Pocketless? Those are indeed Jos's pants. He came directly here from class, when news of my crash spread through the school like wildfire, without changing into decent attire. When Mariana turned up, Jos borrowed a pair of my gym shorts, as well as briefs, but not before Mariana got an eyeful of handsome Jos in the article of clothing under discussion, which in the first instance define how generously he's hung, and in the second, that over two classes this morning he drenched them twice, liberally.

—Jos, Pascal said, Jos. I like Jos.

—Jos likes you. He would have gone ahead and kicked McTaggart, I fear. And McTaggart kicked by Jos would be in the hospital rather than in his rooms waited on hand and foot by the eminent geologist Pascal Raskvinge.

—Nobody would give a hoot if McTaggart sprained both his ankles. Kettle's boiling! Somebody's at the door! Toast is probably burning.

En To Tre

Firstness is such as it is, a mode of being positively and without reference to anything else. Secondness is such as it is, a mode of being with respect to a second but regardless of any third. Thirdness is such as it is, a mode of being bringing a second and a third in relation to each other. I call these three ideas the cenopythagorean categories.

57

—Holger's having a nap, Pascal said. Be quiet.

Jos slipped through the door and closed it softly.

—Hello, Jos, Holger said. I wasn't asleep. Pascal glutted me with marmalade and toast, and I sort of snoozed off.

—I'm back. I went first, as I thought I might be needed here.

—First what? Pascal asked. Help me wash up.

—Never mind what first, Jos said, putting his hand on Holger's forehead. No fever. I could carry you to your bed.

—I'm fine, Jos, Holger said. My only problem is that to walk I have to hop on crutches for a few days.

—I can sleep here, on the floor by your bed, in case you need something in the night.

—Pascal! Holger called. Come and throw Jos out of here.

—Whichwhat? Pascal said, a dishtowel around his neck.

—Explain to Jos that I am not helpless, or senile, or weak as a kitten, and that I intend to live to a ripe old age, please.

—Did I leave my sticky pants here at noon? I'll change back, and return your gym shorts, for the loan of which, thanks, and your briefs, which now smell of inside a girl, and of me.

—Let me see, Pascal said. And come wash cups and saucers.

Synergetics 529.10

It is one of the strange facts of experience that when we try to think about the future, our thoughts jump backward. It may well be that nature has some fundamental metaphysical law by which opening up what we call the future also opens up the past in equal degree.

59

—It's time for another soaking of my wrenched pedal extremity, Holger said. So back to the kettle.

—I'll do it, Pascal said.

—I'll pat on the Liniment of Sloan, Jos said. Official paramedic on the staff of frøken Landarbejder is what I am. She cures by just being here. I could see Holger get better as soon as she rolled up.

—Jos, Holger said, do your pants stay up by faith alone?

—They're stuck on, Pascal said from the kitchen.

—Forgot to zip up. Dick acts as a wedge. Did I forget to say that they're coming to see you, Hugo, Mariana, and Franklin?

—Basin of scalding water! Pascal said. *En garde!*

—I can undo the bandage, Jos. I'm not helpless, if I can ever get you to believe it.

—We like waiting on you, Pascal and I. Put your foot in the water. Cricket, where are the rabbit scuts?

Pascal jogged down the hall, humming the grand theme from *The Reformation Symphony*, and came back with Holger's pyjamas, plaid dressing gown, and one bedroom slipper.

—But, Holger said, there's dinner to hobble to in an hour.

—We're going to bring it to you, Pascal said. Fru Vinterberg will make you a tray, make us all trays, as I told her we had to eat here with you.

—God in heaven, Holger said.

—Off your shirt, Pascal said, and britches and undies. I found the jammies under your pillow.

—What you're doing, Holger said, is playing hospital. Pascal suffocating me with a pyjama shirt while Jos slathers liquid fire on my foot.

—Wrapping the bandage back on is the big thrill, Jos said. Let's get you into the bottoms before I do that. Wonderful aroma, the Liniment of Sloan.

27 Rue de Fleurus

Human nature is not interesting. The human mind is interesting and the universe.

Papyrus

Yeshua was the shepherd who abandoned the nine and ninety sheep to find the one sheep which was lost. There was delight in his heart when he found it, for nine and ninety is a number of the left hand, and if one is added to it, it passes to the right.

62

—Question 1, Comrade Jos, Pascal said, is are you going with me to get our dinner trays in those gummy pants with the snail tracks all over the front, and question 2 is, if you are, how are you going to carry a tray with both hands in your pockets?

—Quite right, O demiliter moral guide. Have to reborrow Holger's briefs and gym shorts. Must look clean-cut and handsome for fru Vinterberg.

—What I fear, Holger said, is that Jos is going to feed me like a baby bird, and put me in the shower afterward, and wash me, and put me to bed with a hot-water bottle.

A Starfish in String

Greek exercises on Hugo's worktable Holger on crutches saw, corrected in Latin, skylight muntins and stiles grid of shadow and square panes, bright, on them, yellow and blue pencils in a James Keiller & Son Ltd Dundee Orange Marmalade jar. Clothbound notebook, Hugo's skilled calligraphic hand. A magazine *Le Petit Gredin*, its cover a meticulous drawing of a scalawaggish urchin with mussed hair, fleshy penis the swarthier for jutting from the pale trace of small swimming trunks. *Centre pour Recherche*, and a little girl with merry eyes on the cover of *L'Espoir*, naked with butterblond hair, genital mound pudgier and more distinctly cleft than Holger would have imagined, *pour une enfance différente*. Manila envelope with Belgian stamps. Franklin's sneakers, mustard and blue, stuffed with white socks, under the table.

64

—Antinoos and Eros, Hugo said. I think I'll sprain my ankle, too.

—Eglund called just now, Holger said, and I assured him that I can stump to all my classes on crutches, and that I'm not in the least out of commission. What we're to make of last night I'm not certain.

—I'm proud of Franklin for insisting that Pascal stay here.

—Well, it went this way after you, Mariana, and Franklin left. Jos absolutely insisted on seeing me safely to bed, tucking me in, putting the crutches against a chair, setting a lamp with tilted shade on the floor for a night light. Then I shooed both rascals out, commanding them to go to bed. I was reading myself to sleep when here came Jos with blankets and pillow, saying that he was going to sleep on the floor by my bed, wearing only one of those sweatshirts of his that seem to have survived unlaundered and unmended as hand-me-downs from his brothers and to have been worn by several strenuous contenders over the last two or three Olympic tryouts.

—Lovely, Hugo said.

—These kippers were cooked by Pascal, who has just left, towed away by Jos. Once Jos, you see, had made his pallet, wrapped in blankets like a red Indian, he remarked casually that Pascal was brokenhearted because Jos had convinced him that the two of them playing field hospital here would be a nuisance rather than a help. So, idiot that I am, I gave him the choice of going back to his room or of fetching Pascal.

—But absolutely, Hugo said. I can't think that Jos was being mean. He just wasn't thinking.

—May I report, for your ears only, that Pascal had been crying when Jos went and brought him in, more or less across his shoulders?

—Pascal, Hugo said, pouring himself a cup of coffee, has obviously existed forever, to look at him, a tall twelve-year-old with the singular, intelligent beauty you see in northern Italians, and is just as obviously growing in front of one's gaze from an awkward, dreamy little boy into a graceful adolescent. Nothing of the ox in him. Father's a diplomat, living apart from his mother, who's some species of psychiatrist. He has depended on his acquisitive mind to stock his heart, and would, I think, be terribly lonely without you and Franklin. He's latched onto you, Holger, because you're all brain, too, and have kept the passion for learning and knowing which is burning so brightly in him.

—Italian? Holger asked.

—Pascal's mother is Genovese. His father's as Danish as a Holstein.

—Pascal was radiant when I woke them this morning, wrapped in the same blanket and with their heads on the same pillow. Foot's much better, I think, by the way.

—Even so, Mariana says you're to stay off it for another two days. The efficacy of Sloan's liniment is largely imaginary, but Papa believes in it, and Mariana. So it works, like everything else they believe in.

Societas Aulus Gellius

If Anders, then Kim. The Alumni Room, regular meeting place of the
Latin sight-reading club, was preempted by old boys and directors, and
Hugo had commandeered the boathouse loft, which the Ungdomsfrihed
Band had made their clubhouse, an oblong white room with red and blue
rafters, square barn windows, bare floor as scrubbed and uncluttered as
a deck. German and Dutch posters for the Cause on the walls, and photographs by Hajo Ortil and Jos Meyer. A red bookcase made by Anders
contained in neat stacks copies of *Signe de Piste*, *Pan*, *Libido*, *Le Petit
Gredin*, *Juvenart*, *Blue Jeans*, and *Pojkart*.

—We sit on pallets, the ones stacked over there, Hugo said. About half of
us belong to both clubs, so it seemed logical to ask to meet here, and everybody agreed.

—Quit looking as if you'll catch something, Harald, Anders said. Nobody's going to put his hand on your knee.

—Why not? Tom said. Harald's knees are nice and boxy.

—Watch it, Harald said.

—So, Hugo said, if we're all comfortable, let's go with line 189 of the Au-
sonius, where the poem becomes Monet, as I was talking about last time,
and Hjalmar has brought two books with Monets that have reflections in
rivers.

—*Glaucus*, Marcus said, is a color adjective, for sure, but what color?

—The color of a river in summer, Harald said, under a clear sky. Green,
blue green, silvery green.

66

—You'd think, you know, Pascal said, that Jos and me in a blanket by
your bed adds up to two, huh? Not a bit of it. Three. Jos, me, and Jos's
hangdown, which didn't.

—Is it having the highest IQ at NFS Grundtvig, Tiger, Jos said, that
makes you warm as a stove?

—I'm not listening to you two, you understand, Holger said, but if I were,
I wouldn't know whether I was hearing grousing or bragging. A little of
good Pastor Tvemunding's snake oil goes a long way, Jos. So, easy.

—Got to get you well. It makes Pascal low in his mind for you to be a cripple.

—Does not, Pascal said. Makes me happy I can help. That's Franklin at the door.

—Hello, Jos Holger Pascal, Franklin said, darting in to shake Holger's hand, touch foreheads with Pascal, and be grabbed, hoisted, and kissed on the tummy by Jos.

—What was that all about? he asked.

—Just feeling friendly, Jos said. Holger and Pascal are shy, being respectively a dignified housemaster and an infant genius, whereas you and I, Citizen Franklin, are rogues, *jo*?

—I shook Holger's hand, Franklin said. And how's your foot? I was forgetting that part of it. Practiced on Mariana. And then Jos, you're to pose at four, Jos, Hugo said to tell you, Jos fucked up my hair, combed it twice. And Pascal and me and Holger are to come to supper at six. I'm to be here with Pascal until then, unless Holger doesn't want us. Then we could go swimming, or something, or something, you know.

—Swimming it is, or the various somethings, Holger said. Off with the two of you.

—Will you be all right? Pascal said.

—No, never. I'll fall out of my chair and get gangrene and die of thirst and loneliness. And take Jos with you.

—I'd thought, Jos said, I'd have a little nap here beside your chair, in case you need something, until four.

67

I crossed the Neva, muddy and in spate, at Vincum, an old town with fine new Roman walls. It was here that the legions trounced a revolt of the Gauls as thoroughly as Hannibal crushed the legions at Cannae years before. The peaceful fields I walked across, sweet with hay and with nothing more than the lowing of cattle and the whistling of larks to ruffle the quiet, were once strewn with black corpses of the Treveri, flocks of carrion birds cawing and pecking.

A deep forest to get through beyond the fields, pathless, dark and thick. Here in the northern reaches of the empire these wildernesses maintain, forests without roads, unmapped marshes, wooded valleys with no human beings for miles and miles. The town of Dumnissus, I knew, lay over to my left, and the springs at Tabernae: lands recently settled by Sarmatians, barbarians brought into the empire to learn farming and to pay taxes.

On the other side of the forest I could see the Belgian town Noviomagus, Constantine's headquarters when he brought the Franks and Alamanni into the peace of Rome. The sunlight after the dark of the forest was wonderful under a blue and open sky, making me for a moment feel that I was in my own country, and half expected to find the vineyards of Bordeaux, steep radiant skies, broad blue rivers, the red roofs of country villas. For the Moselle of the Belgii is the Garonne here in the north, and Roman civilization has made it even more like. Here are Roman vineyards on slopes, green pastures cleared along the river, which is deep enough for ocean vessels, and the tide comes far upstream. This is a watery part of the world, rich in creeks, lakes, springs. No cliffs, no river islands, no shoals. Boats can move freely by current, by oars, by rope and towpath, and the river is fast, unlike the unhurrying, the majestic Garonne with its slow bends and long promontories that impede its progress to the sea. Nor does the Moselle silt up its banks or have swamps of reeds along it. Here you can walk on dry ground to the river's edge. There are even beaches of hard sand, like marble floors, taking no footprint.

A Dial Hand, No Pace Perceived

The tent by lantern light, side flaps down and secure, had the temporized homeliness of nomadic space. The silence of deep dark for Bach, Spartan disregard of the ground's hardness for comfort, accuracy of memory. No depths, Hugo had said, there are only distances. Jos's clinically white jockstrap, that bulked his genitals into a double fist, thumbs out, was the more erotic for being without any decorative line. It remembered archaic basketry, the harmony of its coarse meshwork finely woven, form without style. A little other.

Holger listened to the night, hearing a badger, perhaps, perhaps a stoat. The lake lay as still as mercury.

69

And the river is transparent right to the bottom, where one can see with perfect clarity ribbed and furrowed sand, blue-green watergrasses combed flat by the current but undulant, stitched by zigzagging fish, or clean stretches of pebbles, or whitest gravel with patches of moss. And toward the estuary, seaweed and pink coral, and mussels with pearls, as if nature, which wastes with a prodigal hand, and which owns with indifference all that mankind lusts for, had strewn jewels and the baubles of the rich along the river bottom.

Chub swarm here, a toothsome bony fish, best when cooked within six hours of catching; trout speckled purple and silver; roach, whose bones are not the needles of most fish; grayling, shy and hard to catch. And barbel, who comes down the Saar, a river that rushes through gorges, and is happy, once it has swum past the three-arched Consular Bridge, to be in the calm Moselle. The barbel alone of living things improves in taste with age.

And salmon, with its rose flesh, whose robust tail even at middepth ripples the surface. Who, at a meal of many dishes, has not asked to have the salmon first? Fat, savory, silver-scaled salmon!

And the eel pout is here, too, brought from the Danube to stock another noble river, a welcome immigrant, and one that has thrived. Nature, the master designer, has speckled its back with spots, like the first raindrops of a storm on stone, and each spot she has ringed with a saffron circle. The lower back she has made skyblue. And perch, the only river fish that can vie in taste with those of the sea, delicious as red mullet, and like it filleting easily into halves. And pike, whose local name has given way to the Latin *lucius*, eater of frogs, who keeps to creek mouths and pools, fancier of marshgrass and mud, never seen on the gentry's tables but a frequent fellow in taverns and peasant kitchens, fried golden brown in deep fat. And with him other hardy fish of the people: green tench, and the bleak, favorite of boys at their campfires, and shad, delicacy of the humble hearth, the poor man's salmon or trout. And gudgeon.

And catfish, that genial monster, defying classification. Is it the smallest of the whales and dolphins? Is it the last of a primeval order of nature, living on beyond its epoch?

Friedrichstrasse 1927

Gunther in a secondhand belted jacket the color of oatmeal, a blue pinstriped blouse a size too large, scruffy shoes, wide-brimmed straw hat, short pants. Hair feathery and full at his nape. All of an afternoon Holger had read *Der Puppenjunge*. Hugo had brought it to him, saying that it was a book he ought to know. Narrative is the music of prose, and prose the mute inner thought of poetry. Holger found such statements annoying, neither fact nor theory. They were valuable, however, because Hugo said them. The meaning, Hugo had said, is in the narrative.

71

Look up. Every slope is a vineyard, as if we were in the Campania, Rhodope, or Bordeaux, where our vines are mirrored green in the yellow and silver Garonne.

From the highest ridge down to the Moselle, grapes. The tenders of them shout jovial obscenities to the barges and travelers on the river road. Voices carry over water, and the hills make a natural theater for coarse laughter and rival wit. This *scaena*, a poet might say, includes men half goat and blue-eyed watergirls locking eyes in brambles on the bank, swimming saucily away. Panope, the lady of the river, steals with her daughters, as stealthily as mist at dawn, to nibble grapes, and rude fauns with the gourdish testicles of rams and a bullwhorl of hair between their nubby horns, chase them back into the river. Peasants have seen them dancing all of a summer night, and more, which I will not repeat. *Secreta tegatur et commissa suis lateat reverentia rivis.*

More fit for human gaze is the grove on the hill reflected upside-down in the blue river. The illusion is of trees and vines flourishing deep in the water, swaying with a liquid motion. Barges floating through treetops!

Oars dipping into grapevines!

Sinuous silver slices limb from limb, instantly rejoining them in a rippling dance.

—We should be reading this down at the river, Asgar said.

—Naked, Halfdan added.

And across this inverted landscape comes a battle of boys in skiffs, oars dipping deep, their boats circling each other, the one driving the other into the bank. Workers in the vineyards stop to watch, and cheer their naked sons and brothers on, boys browned by the summer sun, with copperbright hair. When the ships of Caesar Augustus defeated those of Antonius and Cleopatra at Actium, Aphrodite declared games to celebrate the victory at Apollo's temple. She commanded Eros and his stripling friends to re-enact the battle in toy triremes, with tenor shouts mimicking the cries of marines and sailors, and all against a background of the vineyards that slope down Vesuvius, the hanging black cloud of which represented the smoke from burning ships. So the Euboians replay Mylae with charming adolescents in boats. Here on the Mosella, if we look at the inverted reflections of country boys shoving each other's boats with oars, shouting battle cries, we can imagine we are seeing naked Eros playing Roman sailor for Aphrodite's delight, Hyperion embracing them.

And their sisters, watching from the bank, use the river as a mirror to reset the combs in their hair, and to blow kisses to their warping reflections, and wind a curl onto a finger, and study the effect, and complain that their brothers are shaking the river so.

A fishing boat with nets comes along, and boats with men fishing with pole and hook. The boys leave their play to help with the cork-buoyed seines. The catches are laid out, panting and gasping, on the rocks, to drown in air.

72

Whisking rain on the window, weak daylight ruling a stack of thin slits in the blind, the room chill, Jos, rolled in blankets with Pascal on the floor beside Holger's bed, propped himself on his elbows, and craned his neck to see if Holger was, by luck, awake.

—Holger! he said softly.

Pascal ruckled in his sleep.

—Jos? Holger said.

—Half an hour before reveille. The floor has gotten much harder than it was night before last, and twice as flat, and it's cold down here. What about I stick a whippet of a boy in bed with you, followed by myself? Nobody's looking.

—Sure, Holger said.

—I'll take off my doggy sweatshirt, and add our blankets to yours. Pascal smells as sweet as a shampooed and talcumed baby, and has been cooing like one. Is there room on this side? He's sound asleep. I'll huddle in on the other.

—Charming, Holger said.

—Apply an arm around our sleeping friend, or he'll miss me.

—You can keep your sweatshirt on, Jos. I'm not finicky.

—Oo! Jos sighed. It's warm under here, and most of all it's not the hardhearted floor. Listen to the rain.

—Go back to sleep, Holger whispered.

A surge of weightlessness had tossed through his genitals as he slid his arm over Pascal's shoulders. Pascal snuggled his hair against Holger's cheek, and stretched a leg across his thighs.

—It's too nice to go back to sleep, Jos said. Just need to lie here and soak the ungiving floor out of my back and butt, and feel warm and affectionate, and think about people already up and out in the rain. Hugo, about now, is lugging his overworked cock out of a sore and overfucked Mariana, saying his prayers in Greek, to run six kilometers through the wet, singing Lutheran hymns. Franklin's probably with him, hair stuck flat to his head, happy as a piglet at the teat. There are fat and farting politicians out there, dreaming of money. First thing they'll think about when they get up is new ways to steal, start wars, starve the people.

—Starve the people, Pascal said, wrapping both arms around Holger.

—Thinks you're me, Jos said. He gropes, I might warn you. Nothing personal. Dreaming of Franklin.

—Who's dreaming of Franklin? Pascal asked, awake. Hey! Where am I? What is this?

—Good morning, Holger said.

—Holger, Jos said, took pity on us on the hard floor, and has put us in his soft bed, picking us both up at once, you under one arm, me under the other, despite having to hop with us on one foot, and has distributed us around on this supercomfortable mattress, with him in the middle, to keep you from throttling my dick and depraving me.

—How long have we been here? Pascal asked in a small voice.

—All night, Jos said. You had wet dreams the whole time. Couldn't tell which was the rain outside and which the pitterpatter of Pascal sperm under the covers, splashing all over us.

—Good old Jos, Pascal said. Is this all right, Holger? Us in the bed with you?

—Of course not, Holger said. The headmaster would go weak in the knees and have several heart attacks. One boy in my bed would have the same effect on him. And I have, by last count, two.

—Went to sleep on the floor, Pascal said, Jos and me, and I wake up in a bed. Did Jos wake up when you put him in?

—Jos put you in, Holger said. And put himself in. Me, I'm an innocent Icelandic Reformed Evangelical Lutheran, bachelor and hermit, with a tender foot in a bandage, piled all over with naked boys.

—Let's see it with kippers and marmalade, Pascal, Jos said. Eh? Toast and coffee.

He rolled out of bed onto all fours, prowling over to fetch Holger's crutches, which he brought to him ceremoniously. Of his erection he said that it was like his heart.

—Upright and loving God.

73

And along the winding course of the beautiful river country houses sit in orchards.

Once the admiration of mankind was for turbulent and wild waters, such as the strait Sestos faces, the Hellespont, or the treacherous channel between Euboia and Boiotia, where Xerxes crossed into Greece. Now we admire rivers such as this lovely Mosella, where one language flows into another, where merchants, not soldiers, meet, a river narrow enough to talk across.

With what eloquence can I describe the architecture of places? Here are palaces worthy of Daedalos, that man of Gortyna who flew; and temples worthy of Philo who designed the portico at Eleusis; fortresses worthy of Archimedes; and worthy too of the architects in Marcus Terentius Varro's tenth book. Did Metagenes and Ktesiphon of Ephesus inspire the Roman work hereabout, or Iktinus, architect of the Parthenon, who painted an owl of such magical realism that its stare could drive living owls away? Or Dinokhares, who built the Egyptian pyramids which swallow their own shadows and made an image of Arsinoe, the sister and wife of Ptolomaeus Philadelphus to stand in the middle of the empty air under the roof of her temple at Pharos?

All of these might well have built the marvelous structures here in the land of the Belgii, to be ornaments along the Mosella. Here is one high on a cliff, another built out over a bay, another sits on a hill overlooking its vast estate. And here is one flat in a meadow, but with a tall tower. Another has fenced in a portion of the river, for private fishing. What can we say of the many villas with their lawns flowing down to river landings? The marble bathhouses, with steam rooms and swimming pools, where one can see happy and athletic swimmers, some preferring the river itself. A chaster, healthier Naples.

I feel at home among these people, and wonder if the old poetry can picture them, their neat gray villages and winding green rivers, with a proper tone. I have confided in my friend Paulus my misgivings in this matter. Vergil, yes, and Flaccus, their art will serve me, as it has, in making poems of these northern woods. But their center of gravity, to be Archimedean, is in Greece, halfway around the world, and that center is shifting. The young Gratianus, my pupil, and his little brother, know Greece by rumor. It is a fading rumor, and we are moving away from it. This new religion of the imperial family, with its Zeus who was born as a human infant and taught philosophy in a tropical and zymotic province until he was crucified as a common criminal, fits strangely into the order of things. In utmost privacy I have hinted that it is making a prig of Gratianus.

I am myself part Celt, part Roman. The culture of Bordeaux, of which I like to think I am as good an exemplar as one can point to, is a fusion, beautifully proportioned, of Rome and Gaul. Perhaps, as Aristotle says, any two things generate a third, and it is that nameless third quiddity I think I feel in these northern and western reaches of the empire. It is something I see in my Bissula, her braided yellow hair and frank blue eyes. She was a charming slip of a girl when I bought her. Her language was that of the Swabii, and her first lispings of Latin gave me more pleasure than hearing the royal princelings mouthing Greek, their suspicious priest with us in the nursery, cutting his eyes at me if one of our texts alluded to the firm breasts of an Arcadian girl or the hyacinthine hair of a Sicilian shepherd.

Bissula, Bissula, child of the cold and turbulent Rhine. Eyebrows were raised when I freed her. I could not abide the slave's collar around her tender neck. From the slaughterhouse of war, pain, and desolation beyond all powers of a poet to describe, they brought her to me, a promising little scullery maid of a slave, who might also be warm in bed. I freed her before she could know what it feels like to be a slave, and put her in charge of my quarters, diminutive housekeeper that she is, spoiled as she is. The emperor's officious staff can have no notion that she gives me more pleasure to talk to, to watch, to admire for her beauty, than all the princes and fellow grammarians, and these Christiani with their fasts and mystical feasts of magic loaves and wine, among whom I have to move.

The Greek and Roman poets talk about the color of faces, reciting one another's formulae about roses and lilies. By Jupiter! they could do nothing just for Bissula. She has freckles across her nose, like a trout's flanks, and her skin is now clear, like the air itself in the lower sky, now pink, now the brown of breadcrust, when she has been in the summer sun. Her smile is of the north. She is not a miniature woman already skilled in the politics of a family, as in Rome, nor yet a little vixen babbling of fashions in hairdos and romantic alliances, as in Bordeaux and Arles. She is a child.

She has a puppy, name of Spot, and a cat named Grace, and a pet chicken wittily named Imperatrix. She reminds me of my grandson Pastor with his honest eyes and frisky ways. I care nothing for the looks askance and the gossip. She is firmly the mistress of my household. If you want a bottle of Bordeaux, she has the keys to the winecellar on the belt around her trim waist. If you want to be paid for vegetables or a hare, for grooming the horses, my purse is on her hip.

She is, in some sense poets and peasants can understand, but not the corps of diplomats and soldiers with whom I dine and whose rank I share, she is the Mosella. She is the spirit of this land.

At table we talk law and economics, engineering and taxes, politics and Rome. Everything always comes back to Rome, to the Senate and

Caesar. It does not exist, this Rome. It must be made up, hour by hour. Two legions of barbarians who have learned to march and attack in our way: Rome. Paved highways with couriers and goods trains: Rome. And now priests and bishops with their Hades of eternal damnation and their Elysian Fields with golden streets and a gate of pearls: Rome. A bronze eagle on a standard: Rome.

This Rome will melt, as all the others have. The most ancient Rome, the one of red terra-cotta, born of a she-wolf, melted in the pulse of time to become the seven hills ruled by lightning and the entrails of cows, by philosopher kings conversant with gods who lived in the forests and marshes. But this Rome is that of the hobnailed boot, the tax collector, and the new religion from the east, always from the east, one religion after another, Cybele and Attis and the Magna Mater and Mithras, with stranger and stranger rites.

But my Bissula is the world itself, for the world has a soul. It has no tongue, no language, this soul of the world. We live with it in us all our lives, no matter how we try to translate it into laws, violence, arrogance, power over each other, preposterous fables, and ridiculous observances. The political world lurches from slaughter to slaughter. Mankind has become a roost of vultures.

Bissula hates water, and says she should be smeared with tallow under her wool dress. But she is tractable, and I explain in words she listens to gravely, understanding nothing except the music of my voice, that she must be of the new world. Her northern vigor will not be diminished by a Roman bath, nor her desirable toes by sandals. I tell her about the forests of masts in the harbor at Bordeaux, the parks with flowers, the dogs, the streets shaded by trees against the sun, and all of this makes her laugh. *Effulgens.*

74

At Oporto, out in front of the colors, with the fife and the Serjeant Major, he had brought the Eleventh, the bloody Eleventh, down the gangway to *Lilliburlero*, with the sweet fuckers whistling along, for no regiment of foot has ever been formed on God's earth handsomer than a Devonshire regiment.

He had almost got to Salamanca, and had seen sights Hell itself knows nothing of.

And now a roll of drums, and he in his good shirt already drenched and cold with sweat, and the minister with him, and a churchbell ringing the quarter hour. He saw the gallows at which he had not meant to look, with two nooses. He had meant to look only at Ensign Hepburn, who was to die beside him. Why had so many people come to see him die?

He had not slept, had shivered all night, and had puked up the rum the jailer gave him.

The scaffold was in the street, in front of the Debtors' Door, Newgate Prison. In the crowd on both sides of the gallows were Lord Yarmouth, Lord Sefton, and the Duke of Cumberland, the Regent's brother, and Byron's friend Scrope Davies.

The crime for which Ensign James Hepburn, 25, and Thomas White, 16, were hanged on 7 March 1811 had been committed in a room above a public house on Vere Street two months before.

Ensign Hepburn had seen Tom White in St. James Park, and liked the beauty of his sixteen-year-old body enough to send a young friend over to him to sound him as to his willingness to be fondled. Tom White, sizing up Ensign Hepburn, replied that there was a room in Vere Street to which he might be followed. He was fair and well-knit, with a straight back and long stride that had got him chosen as a drummer boy in the Eleventh North Devonshire Fusiliers.

Ensign Hepburn had bought him a pint of bitter and a cold breast of hen between two slices of bread, and these he drank and chewed as his breeches and stockings were removed, with fine compliments for his manly equipment and the firm make of his backside and legs.

And now his eyes were blind and burning, so that he stumbled on the steps. He pulled his sleeves over his wrists.

—Goodbye, Tom, he heard Hepburn say, and he tried to say *Goodbye Jim* but was not certain that the words came out, as in a dream.

While his hands and ankles were being fastened, and the noose fitted over his head, he hoped he was repeating after the minister *For I am the resurrection and the life: he that believeth in me, though he were dead, yet shall he live.*

III

Pascal was still asleep, a bubble between his parted lips, his hair as graceful tangled and matted as when it was combed. Dawn, chill, would give way to summer warmth, a blue sky. Holger, who had expected to sleep tense and anxious, was surprised that he had slept in an easy happiness. Pascal had jabbered, excited and vivacious, in the car all the way to the campsite, as if he had left his solemn composure behind. They had put the tent up well before dark, giving them time to explore and to feel that they were in full possession of their territory.

—We establish a residence, Holger had said, so that this becomes our home, for however short a while.

—Today and tomorrow and the day after, Pascal had said. When I was out with Franklin and Hugo it was like we'd lived there in our camp all our lives, you know, and it was ours. And this is our place. The car, the tent, the lake, the woods. All ours.

— Every bit of it.

—Mama said, How wonderful! And that I didn't need to call Papa.

Holger eased out of his sleeping bag and the tent, stealthily, on all fours. Outside, he dressed in jeans and a sweater. He laid a fire and filled a kettle with water they'd brought.

—Pascal! he called.

—Yo! You're up.

And there he was, knuckling an eye and yawning, in the thin-blue-striped T-shirt and slight briefs he'd slept in.

—Hello hello, he said. Got to pee.

—Anywhere, Holger said. We have the world to ourselves.

—I peed in the ferns last night. Pine needles today. Hugo and Franklin peed together on our outing. They're like that.

—Cinnamon and raisin buns, with butter, with tea, with gnats, for breakfast.

—Being shy is actually pride, Pascal said, facing Holger and making a crystal arc to which he gave a whipped wiggle. Gnats on cinnamon, yum. Lots of milk in my tea.

—We'll go over to that island, shall we, in the boat, once we've squared away?

—The one all blue in the mist?

—That one.

—What's on it?

—Don't know. I've never been over. When I come out by myself I'm content to stay here, wallowing in the quiet and the peace, reading, making notes, with a walk and a swim when I want to. I hope you're not going to find it duller than dull.

Pascal looked out of the sides of his eyes.

—Dull? I'm happy.

Holger chewed awhile and drank a long swallow of tea.

—So am I.

—Is there anybody on the island?

—I shouldn't think so. I'm pretty certain not.

—Then can I go bare-bottom?

—Absolutely.

—Franklin would. And Hugo, to swim. Franklin does it for the fun of it.

— You're wearing a life preserver till we get there. They're in the back seat. I'll get the boat down. We want a jug of water as there's probably no spring on the island, and the net bag, also in the back, for, let's see, bread and cheese and a thermos of tea, the first-aid kit, the binoculars, my notebook.

—I'll put my T-shirt and underpants in too, Pascal said, taking them off, should we meet anybody, I guess.

—And your short pants, friend. And caps for us both.

— You don't mind I'm britchesless, do you, Holger?

—Of course not.

— You're blushing, you know. Real strawberry.

—I'll only blush worse if you keep mentioning it, Holger said. Here, let me get you into the preserver neat and trim. Woof! What's the hug for?

—For bringing me camping.

—Consider yourself hugged back, for coming along, but right now I want you in this cork jacket so securely not even Hugo could rig you better.

—Doesn't matter that I can't breathe?

Holger at the stern, Pascal in the bow, they paddled over to the island, singing *The Owl and the Pussycat*, Pascal looking over his shoulder from time to time to grin.

—In between those two big rocks, Holger said.

Pascal jumped neatly into clear pebble-floored water and pulled the prow onto the shale shingle beach. Holger helped him draw the canoe ashore.

—Rift rocks, very old pines, meadow grass and flora. Wonderfully lonesome, isn't it?

—I like it, Pascal said. Butterflies. How do I get out of this DayGlo-orange straitjacket? Stash the paddles here? If we climb the big rock at the other end we can see the whole island at once, wouldn't you say?

They walked through cool and dark pines in the saddle of the island, coming out on the other side onto a sloped bright meadow that slanted up a sunny shaft of gray rocks where they could see across to the tent and Volkswagen, which looked strangely unfamiliar from this wild vantage.

—A feeling of being very far away is what I have, Pascal said.

—Yes, Holger said. That's why I like getting away. There is decidedly no such place as NFS Grundtvig. Never was.

Pascal laughed.

—Our voices sound different.

—I think we are different.

—Over the edge, said Pascal looking, is steep straight down to the lake. Some enterprising bushes growing right out of the side of the rock. It's nice and hot up here.

Holger sat, unlacing his sneakers.

—The binoculars, Pascal said. Hey, you brought your camera.

He surveyed the full horizon.

—People on the far side. Scouts, I think. Blue and khaki. Tents. They couldn't have come up the road we did.

—You have to know, Holger said, about the gate in the fence, and the cowpath we drove along the last three kilometers, to get to where we are.

Holger pulled his sweater over his head, bare torso beneath, chest hair thick, a gold chain with pendant coin around his neck.

—Why the wicked smile? he asked.

—Not me, Pascal said. What's the medal?

—A tetradrachma, museum reproduction, Artemis and four dolphins, chariot with four leggy horses on the obverse.

Pascal leaned to study it.

—It's beautiful.

—A friend gave it to me. I've worn it for years. You're beginning to turn pink from the sun already.

—You blush, I tan, same shade. We could both tan.

—*You* won't blush, friend? These jeans are all I'm wearing.

—Pride, as I said, is what shy is. Actually, what Hugo said.

Holger stood, nimbly, unzipped his jeans, stepped backward out of them, folded them into a square for a pillow, and lay on the slant of the rock, his fingers knit behind his head.

—Hugo is your real teacher, isn't he? Did we get here with sunglasses? He has caught your imagination.

—Sunglasses, sunglasses, Pascal said, scrounging in the net bag. Thermos, comb, whyever a comb, film, is there film in the camera? bathing suit, my underpants and britches, sunglasses. Here. Can I have your sweater for a pillow? Except that I get the fidgets lying still.

—So don't lie still. Walk on your hands, do jumping jacks.

—Jump you flatfooted, across your chest. One and two and three!

—Good sense of space. I'm not stomped to death and your heels are touching.

—Next, over your belly button. One's all, two's all, zicker-zoll zan! Neat. This is something Franklin would do, you know?

—I've noticed you turning into Franklin.

—Franklin's trying his best to turn into Hugo. I like Franklin. And he's really the only person who's liked me. At Grundtvig, I mean.

—I like you.

—I know that, Holger. Now over your middle. Humpty Dumpty is ninety-nine, and one's a hundred, plop. Over your knees, next, sinctum sanctum buck. Hairy feet. Whoof! Now I can lie down and be civilized. I'm shy.

Holger looked at his watch.

—Another five minutes, and we do our backs.

—Methodical. I like going without clothes. I didn't think I was this kind of person.

—What kind of person would that be?

—I don't know. I really didn't know I had a body until Franklin showed me. It was something my folks owned and operated, not me, something with earaches, constipation, runny nose, clean fingernails, eat your vegetables and drink your orange juice. There's Jos with his muscles and weights and big shoulders, and Rutger and Meg, and Kim and Anders, and Hugo and Mariana.

Pascal sat cross-legged beside Holger, one knee pressing on his thigh.

—Sun and breeze together, Holger said, and such incredible quiet.

—I get kidded a lot because you like me. But it's only kidding, though Franklin had that fight with Adam because of it.

Holger lifted his sunglasses and looked hard at Pascal.

—Jos got Adam the next day and scared the living lights out of him.

—The things I don't know, Holger said.

—But Jos jollied Adam around again. He doesn't like hard feelings.

—I'm not certain I understand any of this.

—What's to understand? Franklin came over, from Hugo's, to see me. Adam, who's a prig, which is what Jos called him, and thinks Franklin is not one of us, and is jealous if you ask me, said something nasty, Franklin won't tell me what, that made Franklin so mad he hit him.

—We should have brought Franklin along.

—Oh no. If Franklin were here, I'd be with him, not with you. That sounds awful.

—Now you're blushing.

—I hear a boat, Pascal said, reaching for the binoculars. It's the scouts, and they're rowing this way, three boats. Come look.

—Our island, Holger said. What wars are all about. Our place that we thought we had to ourselves is about to be invaded. Perhaps if we show them we're here, they'll have the good manners to give us a miss.

—They can see me, Pascal said, nipping over to the net bag for his briefs and Holger's bathing slip. Semaphore flags, he said, for a signal from one naked skinny boy perfectly visible against the sky.

Right arm straight out, flapping briefs, left hand with slip over genitalia: *B*. Both arms up, the body a Y: *U*. Both hands at genital level, a shift to the left: *G*, twice. Left hand up, right over genitalia: *E*. Arms straight out: *R*. Left hand, across chest, right arm up: *O*. Right over genitals, left straight out, twice: *double F.*

—They're answering acknowledge and repeat. Wait a sec. That's a *hello*. They're landing, anyway. Ten, I count. Nine scouts and their keeper.

Holger came to the ledge, hands on Pascal's shoulders to peer down at the boats. Pascal placed his hands over Holger's. Solidarity.

—I suppose we should be grateful that the intrusion is as benign as scouts. Even so.

—Pests, Pascal said.

—Heigh ho! came a jovial voice from the foot of the slope.

—Hello! Holger called down.

The first of the landing party to appear was a freckly ten-year-old in gold-rimmed specs, red bandana around his head, piratically knotted, in short blue pants and webbing belt hung with a canteen and a hatchet. He stopped short, silver braces gleaming in his open mouth.

Behind him arrived an older boy in a beret and red briefs, a mop-haired spadger in sneakers and shorts, carrying a butterfly net, and their scoutmaster, who seemed nineteenish, sturdily athletic, with cropped blond hair and smiling green eyes.

—Thought I ought to apologize, he said, before obeying your semaphore. Also to introduce myself, Sven Berkholst, with my troop. We'll keep to the other end of the island, unless you're camping there.

Nine scouts with fox eyes stood in a line behind him, staring.

—Holger Sigurjonsson. And this is Pascal. We're camped over there on the other side of the lake. We rowed out to see the island, and to have our lunch in a bit.

—Your son?

—Friend. We're both from NFS Grundtvig.

Pascal slipped his arm around Holger's waist, causing elbows to nudge among the scouts. Holger placed both hands on Pascal's shoulders.

—We're from Tarm, Sven Berkholst said. We're out for butterflies, and some elementary marine biology around the shore. Nice meeting you, and we'll push off. Troop, about-face. I'll keep the boys away from up here.

—No need to, Holger said.

Pascal tightened the squeeze of his hug as the scouts left, some looking back furtively. Watching their heads bob among bushes and be lost to sight among the pines, Holger, surrendering to an impulse, hoisted Pascal with a clean swift heave, turned him around in the air, and, clasping him tight shoulder and butt, held him bravely, nuzzling his midriff before easing him down.

—Let's have lunch, Holger said, or whatever midmorning meals are called. Did I do that, hug you, I mean?

—Somebody did. Kissed me on the tummy, too. Why are you putting on your jeans?

—Dressing for dinner, Holger said. It seems sublimely silly to eat in the altogether. Not you, me. Stay in your Adam suit. Bread we have, cheese we have, hot tea with milk we have.

—I'm staying naked all day, Pascal said, especially if I'm going to get hugged. Two plastic cups, cheese in foil, good chewy bread. I thought it was exciting enough getting here yesterday, and putting the tent up, and having our supper, and talking by the fire, and sleeping in a tent, but today, so far, runs rings around all that.

—Oh, I agree, Holger said. This meal, on Hugo's authority, is Epicurean. Epicurus has a bad reputation for high living and outrageous gourmandise. Hugo says, however, that he ate as simply as possible: goat cheese, bread, cold spring water.

—It's good, Pascal said with his mouth full. Hugo hugs Franklin all the time. Mariana makes a joke of being jealous, but of course she isn't, really. Other things, too.

—What other things?

—Just things.

—Clouding over, would you look?

—Good old Danish weather. Drown the scouts, maybe.

—Well, I don't think we'd be that lucky, but I do think we'd be wise to row back to the tent before it rains. Police the area, scamp, and I'll pack.

—Wasn't there, Pascal asked, some chocolate?

—Dessert in the tent. You don't have dessert with a snack, anyway. Thermos, your clothes, such as they are, camera. Wait. Let's photograph you here on the rock. Stand over there. Smile. Got it.

—Can I show the picture to Franklin?

—Why not? Oh boy, is it ever going to rain.

As they crossed the wood they began to hear scouts' voices near the cove where they left their canoe. Smells of turpentine, deep humus, the straw odor of pine needles. The wood was cool and dim, with laurel undergrowth toward the edges, so that one did not suspect the closeness of the lake. Pascal walked in front, the net bag slung over his shoulder. It was the merest chance, as his eyes were happy to keep to Pascal, that Holger took in at a glance, and that peripherally, two scouts in the laurels over to the left. One, with a bearbrown richness of hair raked forward, recurving into a snub-nosed open-lipped profile, had shoved down his shorts and briefs. His penis was rigid, scrotum bunched tight. His head was close to that of another scout, whose hands were busy. Holger kept silent, and for a few steps doubted what he had seen, though the boyish profile and prosperous erection remained as a clear afterimage.

They saw the scoutmaster on the far slope, and waved to him. Two scouts were bottling something, knee-deep in the lake. They secured themselves in their lifejackets, shoved the canoe into the water, and made off. Halfway across, the rain began, soft and swiveling.

—Rain on my peter, Pascal said. That's a new experience.

—And that's something Franklin would say.

—What if I turn into Franklin all the way? Like in science fiction, huh? He's very smart, but hasn't read a great deal, not yet.

—Has it occurred to you, small friend, that Franklin can just as well turn into Pascal, with the highest IQ at NFS Grundtvig, and be voraciously interested in the whole curriculum? I've heard Master Olsen say that he thinks you're doing Jos's algebra for him.

—A swap, Pascal said over his shoulder, looking around with flat wet hair. I do his algebra and he lets me see his magazines.

—I'm not asking what kind of magazines, not out in the middle of a lake, wet to the skin, with waves beginning to chop.

—You don't want to know, friend Holger. Boys are nasty.

—That's why I have to get away to the woods for a few days every month.

—And bring one boy with you. I hope it's dry in the tent.

—There's nothing cozier than a tent when it's raining, as you'll see in two shakes of a lamb's tail. Hop ashore and steady the prow.

They unrolled the sleeping bags to sit on, and Holger wrapped Pascal in a blanket from the car before he stripped and dried, put on an outing shirt and pyjama trousers.

—The scouts should be thoroughly soaked by this time, Pascal said.

—No wetter than us. Is your hair drying? You look like a baby bird in its nest, with only your face and frizzled hair outside the blanket. So much for going bare-assed all day.

—I'm naked in the blanket, if that makes any sense. Feels good, a rough blanket. I feel good, anyway. I'll bet you didn't see two scouts over to our left when we were crossing the pinewood, taking off each other's pants.

—I did, as a matter of fact. Mostly out of the corner of my eye, but an eyeful nevertheless.

—They had stiff peters, you mean.

Holger answered with a forgiving shrug.

—Our place, Pascal said. Our tent. We're dry after being wet, warm after being cold, and we're all by ourselves after uninvited pests.

The rain quit midafternoon. They explored the deep wood on their promontory, Pascal wearing a sweater and sneakers only. They found a wildflower Holger could not identify, and a moss and fern of uncertain name. Pascal gathered leaves to press and learn. They peed together, mingling and crisscrossing streams. When Holger was laying the fire for supper, Pascal gave him a generous hug from behind.

—I'm being silly.

—I don't think so, friend Pascal.

—I don't even hug Franklin. We josh and grab each other.

—You're lovely, you two.

Pascal puffed out his cheeks in bemused puzzlement.

—Hugo says we're pukey, and Mariana, depraved.

—That's affectionate teasing.

—I know that. But Pastor Tvemunding, Hugo's papa, said like you that we're lovely. Jonathan and David, he said we were. That set Hugo off. He

and his papa talk about everything: it's wonderful. They know the Bible
off by heart, in Hebrew and Greek, and history and science. They make
everything seem different. And they're very funny. They can sit and read
each other things out of the newspaper and books, and set each other
laughing. Franklin says it's some kind of code, and we've never figured out
what they laugh about. Pastor Tvemunding says the Devil has no sense of
humor whatsoever, and that you can always get his goat by laughing. Me,
I asked him if he really believes there's a Devil, and he cocked his head, cute
old man that he is, and said that the Devil's only claim to existence is our
belief in him.

—What do you suppose he means by that?

—Hugo took over, and said that the Devil is precisely nothing.

—Soup in a cup, Holger said. And sandwiches of any of these, in any or
all combinations.

—Sardines and cheese. Hard-boiled eggs. Franklin would love a sandwich of a chocolate bar and sardines. Soup's good.

—I'll light the lantern in a bit, and we can move into the homey tent, out
of this damp. And snap the flaps closed, as I'd say it's going to rain again.

—Terriff, Pascal said, his mouth full, and super. You got some sun, you
know.

—I also know that neither of us has had a bath today.

—Do we have to?

—This is our weekend for doing what we want to. But we'll wash up
these supper things in the lake, and pick off some of the pine needles stuck
to your behind and brush our teeth.

The tent by lantern light was snug. Fog had risen on the lake and a soft,
meditative rain made a whispery rustle against the tent.

—In the buff all day, Pascal laughed, here I am putting on pyjamas to go
to bed.

—Life's like that.

—Wildly illogical.

—What a fine sound, the rain.

Holger with his jeans and sweater for a pillow, Pascal sitting cross-
legged, they talked about the island, its geology and vegetation, the scouts
across the lake, the freckles on Franklin's nose, Paul Klee, Icelandic ponies

and meadows, Holger's briefs, the label of which Pascal held to the lantern to read, double stars, Kafka, toenails, zebras, Jos Sommerfeld's symmetrical physique and asymmetrical mind, butterflies, the depth of the lake, Pascal's mother, Hugo and Mariana, masturbation, causing Pascal to slide his hand into his pyjama pants with an impish look of greenest innocence, the fight between Adam and Franklin, irrational numbers, petals and sepals in crocuses, whether Iceland is the first part of the New World to be settled by Europeans or the westernmost country of Europe, what it means that friends are another self, as Pastor Tvemunding says, Hugo's room over the old stables, its photographs and paintings and the organization of its space, and what make of microscope Pascal should inform his father to buy for him, as promised.

—And if we're going to be up early tomorrow and explore the other side of the wood, or maybe go back to the island, we should douse the lantern and listen to the rain and get some sleep, wouldn't you say? What are you doing, mite?

—Taking off my pyjama bottoms.

Holger, on his knees, extinguished the lantern.

—Now what are you doing?

—Getting into your sleeping bag with you.

IV

Paulus' Brev Til Efeserne VI.12

Thi den kamp, vi skal kæmpe, er ikke mod kød og blod, men mod magterne og myndighederne, mod verdensherskerne i dette mørke, mod ondskabens åndemagter i himmelrummet.

77

—Liked having breakfast with you this morning, Jos said. All that neatness. You could run a hospital or a submarine. And Pascal neater than you. And the good talk. Is it awful I'm jealous, or envious do I mean? Napkins, real cloth napkins.

—Everybody's to get a breakfast, Holger said. The vulnerable meal, but with built-in leaving time.

—With Pascal at all of them? You're becoming Hugo for dash and facing down Eglund.

—I run before breakfast, Pascal, Hugo, Franklin, and I. I write before breakfast. Plan classes. The things one learns on a morning run.

—You're becoming me.

—Like now, lifting weights.

—You're really going to the boathouse to lay a talk on the revolutionaries?

—Sexiest part of you, Jos, is the way your top lip makes a beveled wedge in the middle. And your back. Like your back.

—Conversation stopper if ever I heard one. No, I can return the serve. It never gets me anywhere to say something like that to you.

—Count.

—Sixteen more. Looking good. I'm making you and Pascal do the same routines, you with more iron.

—Turning into Pascal, too. An article on Carl Sauer accepted, American geographer.

—Good hollow scoops on the outsides of your butt: leg lifts and running to keep them that way. Wicker chairs, Cretan shawl, flowers in a vase, bowl of roses. Nicest room in all Grundtvig, you know. Thorvaldsen and Kierkegaard on the wall.

—They make a chord. Hugo opted for Georg Brandes and Kierkegaard. He says they solved for Denmark the social and psychological problem of inside and outside.

—There, sixteen. What the fuck is inside and outside?

—Inside is the privacy of the imagination, which the Bible calls the heart, where the fool has said there is no God and where one can be angry with one's brother, secretly, and be a murderer, and lust after a deer-eyed woman and be an adulterer.

—Bullshit, Jos said. Hook your feet under the strap and do fifty sit-ups with your hands behind your head, knees well bent.

—The invisible heart has always been a hard place for moralists. The church has always tried to monitor and censor it. So has psychiatry, and fru Grundy, parents, and other busybodies. Hence our search for new kinfolks. We find them most of all, Hugo says, in people who can make their inside outside, that is, artists and poets, sculptors and composers, who moreover have the ability to show us our own insides, our imagination.

—Don't jerk when you lift. Make one clean deliberate movement. If you made a movie of my imagination, you couldn't show it even in Denmark. Germany, maybe, but they wouldn't appreciate it, being nerds.

—All meaning is narrative. Hugo, again. So we Danes decided, following Kierkegaard and Brandes and others, that we could tolerate everybody's inside difference provided we all respected that difference, and made the respect an outside sameness. That's why you can roller-skate around the parkering and the peripheral road with your dick out through the fly of your jeans.

—Heard about that, have you? Have to keep them on their toes, you know.

—Franklin told it at supper, admiringly.

Enten Eller

—All systems, like Kierkegaard's thought that anhelates toward the paradox of the unthinkable, Jos said, have hiccups of chaos in them, as turbulence is new information and a specific against entropy. Do I, or don't I, sound like Pascal?

—Very Pascal, Pascal said.

—More like Pascal, Holger said, than Pascal.

—So these wide-eyed revolutionaries with their den over the boathouse who treat Sebastian as an ichneumon.

—Catechumen, Pascal said.

—Whatever. I took him, high-handedly, as you can't go without a comrade. High-handedly, as I'm not a member myself.

—With your and Sebastian's jeans and underpants rolled under your arm.

—Very Gray Brothers. Kim was in stitches.

—Franklin is right, Holger said. Sebastian would find Hugo's wolfcubs more exciting.

—It's the principle of the thing, Jos said. How was I to know that Anders was going to read a paper on the architecture of grebes' nests? Made of sticks on the water. At least Sebastian thought that was neat, and has been talking grebes ever since. They run on the water, grebes, like Jesus in a hurry.

—Go back to your being pantsless.

—Grand success. Everybody followed suit, once we'd heard about grebe sticks. Tom then gave the news from around the world on what Fascist government has passed what laws against who can hug and kiss whom, and where. Lard butts with terminal halitosis in Washington who are willing to kill every man, woman, and child on the planet with napalm, poison gas, and hydrogen bombs, write laws against taking your dick out even to piss. So I joined them then and there, Sebastian too, contraband as he is. I don't even like Sebastian, much less love him. That's when Tom had a laughing fit, as it turns out that Sebastian had already joined, twice before, in fact, once with Franklin as his bonded mate, and once with Pascal, ditto.

79

The wooded knoll above the bend in the river, a Chekhovian place, wicker beehives just beyond the hawthorns, a tinge of honey in the light. Franklin, nothing shy, at least offered authority for his presumption.

—Pascal said.

He had grabbed and fought his arms into the sleeves of a hooded jacket as soon as Holger had said he needed a ramble.

—Me too, Franklin had said, causing Hugo to look at the ceiling.

—New style, holding hands. Jos said it's sissy, and then he held hands with me across the quad. He'd also just put down kissing as perverted, and then smooched Sebastian on the mouth. Butterscotch and foreskin he said it tasted like.

—What happened to Sebastian's hair? Holger asked.

—Well, Franklin said, I cut it. Looks good, wouldn't you say?

—Franklin, it looks awful.

—Never cut anybody's hair before. There was general opinion at the clubhouse that he had too much of it, and that he would look less like a girl with about half of it scissored off. Guess I got more than half, didn't I? Pascal cut a pair of his jeans off good and short for him. Now the pockets show.

—Could you find Sebastian, do you think, when we get back?

—Sure. What for?

—To take him to the barber. And, friend Franklin, if I sent you and Pascal to Jorgensen's on the bus, would you get Sebastian a pair, two pairs, of niggling britches with a snide fit, like yours?

Franklin made his face a rabbit's by rucking his upper lip, catching the nether under his wedgy teeth, rounding his eyes, and wrinkling his nose.

—We could, you know, get him some tough sneakers, too, and ballsy socks.

—Better and better.

—And some underpants that don't sag or come up over his belly button.

—You're being brilliant, friend Franklin. And how will he take all this? Will it hurt his feelings?

—Might, at that, come to mention it. Pascal can say he's sorry he ruined his jeans. He'll think of something, too, for the sneakers and socks and nappies.

—Just what is going on with Sebastian?

—Like at the clubhouse? He hasn't a clue what the meetings are about, making two of us, as I don't either, when it's my turn to go with him. I mean, book reports! An old fart from England bleating about what's against the law in Germany or Belgium. In *engelsk*, to boot. He wanted to interview, he called it, Sebastian, who he'd been staring at all along, maybe because of his haircut but probably, wouldn't you say, because he looks as if he's escaped from his babysitter. Didn't Pascal say you were coming some Wednesday soon?

—How does anybody get around Pascal?

—You don't.

—You'll be fun, like the loony Dutchman we all peeled to the knackers for, and who kissed us, hilarious, and grew a bone. I'll find out what they did after they threw me and Sebastian out. Tom and Kim, the two I've asked, answered with a shitty smile.

—Pascal wants me to talk about time and territory.

—Sounds as sexy as Matron in hair curlers.

—The body as a territory and as an organism in time. The body as narrative and event. As figure against a ground, against history. Wittgenstein in an intriguing *Zettel* comments on the surface temperatures of the body, without particulars. Cold elbows, warm armpits.

—Hugo hollers about Mariana's cold feet.

80

—Really should have brought Barnabas, Franklin said. But Mariana would have had to come along too, for him to drink from. And if Mariana, Hugo, to fuck Barnabas a little sister. Find one thing wrong with this tent, Sperm Breath, and we'll see my footprint on your butt for the next two days.

—Right back peg's not in line, Pascal said. I'll mention it before Holger does. Oof!

—Warned you.

—Boys, Holger said.

—The last weekend that can be called summer, Pascal said, by any stretch of the imagination. You'll like the foul-weather times, friend Franklin. We've even been crazy enough to go over to the island with rain coming at us sideways by the bucketload, and inside the tent is wonderful when there's a nasty drizzle.

—Which is what we'll get when and if we talk Holger into bringing us out

with Alexandra, some Friday, returning on Sunday afternoon to collect
the limp bodies, eyes rolled back in our heads, sweet idiots.

—There's got to be a weekend, Holger, when you've had it with Pascal,
can't stand the sight of him, and will be all for hauling us out here. Won't
need to provide anything but transportation and tent. We won't eat.

—The contingency, Holger said, will have to be something else, such as
my generosity, or simply because I can't say no to Pascal.

—Hugo and Mariana are always saying they'll sell me to the Gypsies,
first offer. Sometimes it's give me to the Gypsies. But it would take Israeli
Commandos to pry Holger loose from Pascal.

—Aren't you sort of forgetting, Holger said, that you and Pascal can,
without a word or sign, get each other's britches off? When was it, last
Tuesday, I was grading papers, Pascal was typing at the desk, his back to
Franklin, who was lettering in his map assignment on the floor.

—Good afternoon, Pascal said. Grace abounding.

—Agreed, but Franklin sat up, watercolor brush in teeth, unbuttoned his
jeans, and went back to making the Balkans green and yellow. Then Pascal, between shifts of the carriage, undid his belt and when he could spare
a hand, kept edging his zipper down. The *a* of Bulgaria finished to his sat-
isfaction, Franklin stretched prettily in the afternoon sun, with a sunny
smile for me, serious thoughts in his eyes, which I took to be about the geography of the Balkans.

—Holger, Pascal said. You were supposed to crook your finger, and get
climbed all over.

—Well, I, at least, was thinking geography. So Pascal quit typing, slid out
of his chair as casually as you please, and without so much as a half glance
over his shoulder, walked backward until his butt was against the back of
Franklin's head. I saw all this with my own eyes. Then the two of you had
your jeans and underpants off in something under three milliseconds, and
in three more were wrapped around each other on the floor.

—Could be, Franklin said, we're horny all the time. Fact is, though, I
mean aside from being horny all the time, we know what the other's
thinking. Like what flavor of ice cream. It's not done to have to ask. We
never miss.

—Holger's only pretending he can't read our minds. Mariana can.

—I can't, though, Holger said.

—We can teach you, Franklin said. Look. I'm closing my eyes. Better, Holger's going to blindfold me with a handkerchief or something. And bang two pans together so I can't hear footsteps. Pascal's going into the woods, out of sight, so Holger, even, won't know where. Then I'll walk right to him, OK?

—Challenge taken, Holger said. This is going to be good.

—I warn you, Holger, Pascal said. He can do it.

—Of course he can't do it, Holger said. I'm tired of these irrationalities in students I'm trying to teach science.

Pascal shrugged and trotted off as Holger was tying his handkerchief across Franklin's face. He tiptoed for a while, doubling back from entering the undergrowth to sneak along the edge of the lake. Here, he took off his shoes and socks and waded some meters out, thigh-deep. Holger the meanwhile clashed two frying pans close to Franklin's head. At a signal from Pascal, he said:

—Ready. Go find him.

Franklin stood still for a full two minutes.

—Untie my sneakers, he said. You'll think I'm peeping if I bend over.

Barefoot, he did an about-face and walked toward the lake, off course by ten degrees at first, correcting with confidence as he walked. At the water's edge he felt around with his foot before striding in.

—Fuck, he said cheerfully.

Approaching at a different angle than Pascal's, he waded through deeper water, up to his belt.

—Really shitty of you, you know, he said, hugging Pascal.

—OK, Holger called. I'm sending back my diploma to the university. Hey! Watch it!

Franklin with a sturdy shove pushed Pascal under the water, to be himself pulled under by a thrashing Pascal. Muddy and sodden, they walked hands over shoulders to shore, spitting lake water.

—Wring everything out, Holger said. I'll put up a clothesline while Franklin tells me how he did it.

—I knew where he was, Franklin said.

—But how?

—Knowing is knowing. We've got goose bumps.

—Towel, Pascal said, tossing one.

Holger caught the towel in the air, and began drying Franklin with a rough swiftness, the quicker to get to Pascal.

—Work on your hair some more with the other towel, Holger said, and wrap the blanket around you.

—Save room for me, Pascal said.

Holger, having run a spare tent rope through the belt loops of their wet hiking shorts, the arms of their jerseys, and the leg scyes of their briefs, tying the rope between two birch saplings, discussing Franklin's prescience with, as he said when he looked over his shoulder, the woods, lake, and sky, finished to find Pascal and Franklin rolled tight in their blanket, all but the tops of their blond heads.

—Kissing, Franklin said, except that I can't see that it gets you anywhere. Crawl in with us, Holger.

81

Over the summer the hallway between Holger's living room and bedroom had been restructured into a large, square study with two glass walls. This elegantly modern extension was into a small garden surrounded by a brick wall high enough to make the study a private and sunny room. Bookshelves had been built from floor to ceiling on one of the walls that was not all window, and a Rietveld worktable, three by two and a half meters, stood along the other. A glass door opened onto the flagstone terrace. This renovation was Hugo's idea, and design, agreed to by Eglund, paid for by the Alumni Fund.

—The corridor, Hugo had said, will grow sideways and be a third large room, its darkness becoming a splendid cube of sunshine and airiness, with an inside-outside feel.

—And, Holger said, it is ten times lovelier and sweeter than I could picture it. It is, quite simply, wonderful.

—Well, Hugo said, all I had to do was remind Eglund, who's nobody's idiot, that your geography book, and the edition of Horrebow, would precipitate offers from universities and other schools. I kept silent about your decision to lead a scholarly and circumspect life at Grundtvig.

—But, Holger, dear soul, what with your being chosen to be headmaster once Eglund retires, all the money in the world, nor all the prestige, could entice me away.

—*Lovelier, sweeter, wonderful,* Hugo said. Three non-Icelandic words uncharacteristic of your diction, as was.

—Have I changed so much?

— Yesterday, when you were watching, and helping, Franklin and Pascal change Barnabas, you were as different, advanced is what I mean, from the Holger I first knew, as a tree laden with apples from its sapling. The four of you were of an average age, which would be what, thirteen, Barnabas's one rather bringing it down. And after all the promiscuous kissing of Barnabas, spout and all, you pleased Mariana tremendously by sitting with your chin on her knee to gaze at Barnabas at the teat.

—Beautiful breasts Mariana has. Barnabas is Eros himself. Those eyes!

—Barnabas thanks you for the compliment, but begs to second his father in noting that if there's a clone of Eros about, it's Pascal. Does he glow in the dark? I overheard one of the new kids pointing him out to another. The argot in which they parsed his beauty I'll spare you, but the rest was that he publishes articles in journals his teachers can't get published in and gets taken on long trips by the biology and geography master.

82

Cornflowers and red valerian in a marmalade jar. Rye biscuits, cheese, red Dubonnet. Wet autumn leaves stuck to the glass walls of Holger's studio.

—Pascal's making a happy idiot of me released all kinds of energies, Holger said. I began a notebook at the beginning of the summer, after discovering Auden's *Letters from Iceland,* seeing that there's a species of writing where any and everything fits in. So that's what I've done, as you've seen. I've tried, Hugo, to follow your injunction to write exactly what I wanted to. So my work on arctic mosses, the essays on Sereno Watson and Sauer, fossil flowers and insects, are in with Pascal's toes.

—Nice toes, Mariana said, but not as sexy as Franklin's.

—Please don't get us tossed out on such a cozy afternoon, Mariana sweet, Hugo said.

— You can stay, Holger said, as long as Barnabas is so blissfully asleep.

—You hold him better than Hugo, Mariana said. Hugo is likely to look up something in the dictionary, with Barnabas upside-down under one arm. He's not wet, is he?

—Have we pissed ourselves, Tiger? Not us. We're dry and aromatic: talcum and hyacinths.

Hugo leafed back and forth through Holger's manuscript.

—Samuel Johnson in the Hebrides. Lavas, gannets, mosses. Pascal's knees. Doughty in the Finnmark. *If we look to nature, we see nothing human, and if to the human, nothing natural.* Baltic islands, their wildflowers and butterflies. Pascal's eyes. Iberomaurusian harpoons. Jeremy Bentham. Icelandic trolls.

—Trolls in a bramble I had to pass on the way to school, Holger said. I became convinced that there were elves in it who would do me a mischief if I didn't think kindly of them as I drew near. They are the opposite of Pascal. Over the summer something changed in me that's so peculiar I don't know what it is. I was taken apart and reassembled in a new geometry. Suddenly I could talk and write in a new way. I have stopped the car to make notes of ideas, have dictated to Pascal while driving. Better still, I've allowed Pascal to do some of the writing. He says he can read my mind, and that there are things which he says I know the trolls in the bramble will get me for writing, which he has written for me, like the paragraph about tongues under foreskins, just after John Burroughs on winter sunshine and squirrels. And before Goya and the humanity of children.

—That's Franklin with the freckles, Mariana said, and warty knuckles and round-eyed gaze at his dink when he's galloping it, and who believes that if he doesn't jack off at least thrice a day he'll go into a decline and waste away, and that six times a day keeps him sound and happy.

—Pascal is my daimon. Franklin, Pascal's.

—Who's Franklin's? Hugo asked.

—You, Mariana said. And you have more daimons than can be counted. Your father, handsome Jos, your scouts.

—No, sweetheart, Hugo said. You. You and Barnabas, now that he's here.

—Hello, Barnabas, Holger said. Decided to open your big blue eyes, did you?

—In which that wondering look, Mariana said, means that he's having a serious pee. Aren't you, Lamb?

—I'll change him, Holger said. I'm not as good at it, yet, as Franklin and Pascal, but Barnabas doesn't seem to mind.

—He likes Bedstefader Augustus most of his admirers. He has a Faroese magic charm he chants to mesmerize Barnabas into cooperation. Misses having his dink kissed and trifled with by Pascal and Franklin, though.

—Do I change in the manner of Pastor Tvemunding or of F. and P.?

—Go for Pascal's style, Mariana said. It's our big afternoon out with Holger and cheese and crackers and potent Dubonnet. And if I read Hugo's mind accurately, he's planning to leave Barnabas here for the next hour or so, to provide him with a little sister, or brother, or both.

—Besides, Hugo said, I see a long brown leg coming over the wall, and a blond head and able arm, Pascal as ever was.

—They do that, Holger said. Means there's another. Handsome leg over first is achieved by Jos's or Franklin's back. Otherwise you see hands first, then head, a knee, and you have a boy in your garden.

—It's Jos, Mariana said, wearing Pascal's cap. What a leap!

—Thus the use of gymnastics, Hugo said, to fly gracefully over a wall into your housemaster's garden.

They mimed idiotic delight, peering in through the glass wall, wiggling fingers at their ears, cross-eyed, tongues stuck out.

—Hruff! Pascal said, rotating through the door, we've lucked onto Mariana with the giggles in her eyes, lucked onto Hugo full of cheese, crackers, and Dubonnet *rouge*, lucked onto Barnabas with his dick on the snoot. Are all babies' balls so fat?

—Come on, Hugo, Mariana said. Barnabas can tell us the rest of this when he learns to talk.

—Gym, Jos said. Pascal did a triple set of fifty presses without a gasp. Whack his tummy and break your hand. Feel the definition of his pectorals.

—Me, too, Mariana said. Why, Pascal, are you in Jos's hopeless sweatshirt that's parting at the seams on the shoulders and that a billy goat would think was his father?

—Because he let me. Also his jockstrap with the mesh pouch, see, and his ratty socks. Not for the finicky.

—Holger, Mariana said, darting a teasing glance at Pascal's happiest of grins, if Barnabas stages a tearing snit, send him over by whoever's coming our way. Quick, Hugo, before Pascal takes everything off.

—I see what you mean, Hugo said.

—Barnabas couldn't care less. He thinks he's joined the navy.

—I'll walk you over, Holger said.

—We're not walking, Hugo said. We're running.

—Fine and dandy, Jos said. Off to place an order with the stork. Would you look, friend Barnabas: as soon as your mummy and daddy are out the door, here's Pascal, bosom friend of Uncle Franklin and all of whose clothes seem to have fallen off, butting the crotch of Holger's jeans, and getting a subarctic glare for it.

—The *huldufolk*, Pascal said, are in the bramble, looking out with elvish eyes.

—And, Holger said, gathering Pascal into a comprehensive hug, the owl is in her olive.

—Holger, Jos said to Barnabas, was born and raised in Iceland, where neither the sheep nor the Lutherans approve of sex, and make rather a long face when it intrudes into their decent daily round.

—Crazy horny, Pascal said. Jos's sweatshirt is magic. It belonged to his brothers before he got it. Smells of all three of them. Has Jos sperm all over it.

—How do you put a baby to sleep? Jos asked. Don't you bounce it on your shoulder, or something, while humming Brahms?

—Let me show you, Pascal said. You put his head like this and jiggle him gently, gently, and recite Vergil or the yellow pages, he doesn't care which. He'll either drift off to sleep or stick his fingers in your eyes. Sometimes he pukes into your collar.

—Sweet little buggers, babies. It looked for a while this summer that I'd made one on Suzanne, and one on Fresca. If Rutger could get pregnant, I'd have had to sweat him out, too. False alarms. God is kind to idiots.

—Rutger, Pascal said.

—We did two weeks of backpacking in Germany, Black Forest and around. Youth hostels. Wildflowers. Swedes with big blue innocent eyes fucking all night, squish squish. Awesome silences at noon. There was this girl who.

—I've heard all that, Pascal said, and I believe some of it. Tell about Rutger.

—Not with Barnabas listening. Look, if you two want to fall on each other, ease Barnabas into my arms and we'll have a nap here in the sun on the floor, or take him down to my room. Rutger has probably never seen a baby. Sebastian will like him. Would Barnabas enjoy being jacked off?

—Are you certain, Jos, Holger asked, that you know how to hold a baby?

—No, but I can learn real fast.

—Your shoulder's his pillow, Pascal said, and your arms and chest his cradle. Cradles rock. So rock him sweetly, like this. Hum *A Mighty Fortress Is Our God*, and he'll think you're Pastor Tvemunding.

—Crazy. Will he piss me?

—That'll mean he loves you. I hear Holger turning down the bed and zipping down his jeans. Jos?

—Hello, Barnabas. Like me, huh? Yes, Tiger?

—Shall I?

—I'll hold my breath.

Pascal, padding down the hall, stopped, spun on his heel, returned to kiss Barnabas on the cheek and Jos on the mouth.

—Local custom, he said, trotting off.

—Lucky bastard, Jos said to Barnabas, having Mariana for your mummy. And handsome me for your babysitter. And Holger the Icelandic Lutheran and the wizard Pascal, though those two are this very minute licking each other in susceptible places, and being wonderfully friendly and tender. And now the rousing stanzas of *A Mighty Fortress Is Our God*, as sung by Jos Sommerfeld, Eagle Scout.

Arise O captives of starvation!
Arise O wretches of the earth!
For justice thunders condemnation.
A better world's in birth.

It is the final conflict,
Let each stand in his place.
The International Party
Shall be the human race!

—Jos! Holger said, looking around the door, with Pascal behind him.

Arise O workers of the world!
Throw off the foul disgrace!
And the International Party
Shall be the human race!

—Isn't it a grand tune! Comrade Barnabas says I'm the only babysitter he'll be a good boy for, here on out.

—Jos.

—Huh?

—Jos, Holger said, come on back, with us. Give me Barnabas.

Pascal, fiddling with the drawstring knot of Jos's sweatpants, said:

—Where do you learn such knots? From sailors?

—Knackers never been tighter, Jos said. Pat Pascal on the rump after gym, get butted in the tummy by his sweet lovely head, grope him and get groped before climbing the garden wall, and you find yourself in Holger's bedroom, and bed, I hope.

—Tilt the lampshade, Holger said, so the light's not in Barnabas's eyes.

83

Holger, spent, recited genera and species of Norwegian forests, asking between *Betula pendula* and *Fraxinus excelsa* if there were any cold bubble water a handsome boy might bring him.

—In a sec.

—I'll get it. You're busy.

—Hooked. That Italian town that was so green and open in its piazza, buildings so mellow and sunny, where we arrived one noon. If you're finding bubble water, I need a sip. You went to find us a room with matrimonial bed, as they say, the Italians, and I checked out the magazine kiosk and had a pee in the shady corner of a wall, observed by an appreciative old gentleman around the side of his newspaper. Well, there you were across the square, and it hit me, one of those sudden flip-flops of the mind, that this was the longest distance we'd been from each other in maybe a month, you know, and that you were Holger Sigurjonsson, from Iceland, geography and botany master at NFS Grundtvig, needing a haircut, wearing khaki shorts and sneakers without socks, and a tank top with the

Dansk Ungdoms Fællesråd insignia on it, and you were smiling, blissfully happy. And, this is the spooky part, you were a bit unfamiliar, a stranger for a second or so, someone I couldn't place right off, and so was I, seeing my reflection in a shop window, a sprout of a boy whose feet seemed too big, legs too long, also needing a haircut, probably going crazy from hyperejection of sperm, blue smudges under my eyes, but more likely becoming a moron from being too happy. And there you were, walking across the square, drenched in Italian sunlight, somebody I knew but couldn't quite place. You ever have such moments?

—All the time. Heart skips a beat every time I see you. I'll do odd things on the tennis court, and Hugo sighs and smiles. Shall we resume our game, he doesn't need to say, when Pascal is out of sight?

—Awful.

—There was a blind folksinger in Iceland when I was your age. He lived on a farm with his sister and brother-in-law. An uncle who knew him used to take me out for a day in the country from time to time. He would ask me to describe meadow flowers, colors and shapes and distribution over the pastures. He could remember them from before losing his sight. I would pick them for him to feel and smell.

—So you're a botanist. Poor fellow, the blind man.

—A sweet, gentle man. With a fine voice and a great repertory of songs, probably medieval, some of them.

—A good photograph that would make, Pascal said, the slats of late afternoon light across the bedtable. Underpants, the book of Isak Dinesen's flowers, one sock. Russian Constructivist, all the diagonal lines. Tell me more about the blind folksinger.

Yellow Maple, Autumn Mist

Alexandra, blue silk scarf fluttering at her throat, was on the far side of the soccer field, white jeans, red sweater, in dialogue with Franklin by arm semaphore. Pascal, coming from the gym, hair wet, sneakers fashionably untied, joined in. Franklin to Pascal. Pascal to Alexandra. Alexandra to both.

—Kære gud! Jos said to Holger. Did you read that?

—Afraid so.

85

Across a slant and mellow radiance a spider had knit her web in the barley. Further along, grebes foraging. Holger thought of the mosses and gannets of Iceland, of *huldufolk* in a bramble, of Pascal at sixteen, at twenty, how handsome he would be. Shared time doubles.

Charles Ives: Strygekvartet Nummer 2 (1907–1913)

A smiling Jos said after the concert by the Copenhagen String Quartet in the auditorium that however the music went down with the Grundtvig smart set and all the townies they at least got to see him in a jacket, shirt and tie, Sunday trousers, and shoes. Hair combed, too. Shirt and tie were Rutger's, but the rest was his own togs.

—Not only me in my finery, but in Holger's company. Didn't believe it when you asked me. Underwear and socks, Rutger's, too. Tie clasp. Did I behave?

—Exemplary, Holger said. And seemed to like it, even.

—O ja! Love fiddle music. Got to pee.

—Here?

—Not to play the game. Modesty's pride. Pride's class hegemony. Very bad, according to Nils.

—*Kære Gud!* Hugo said, coming over from the dispersing crowd, the Ives, the Ives! Every so often something other than Whitman, cornflakes, and blue jeans comes out of the USA. I'm not saying a word, you'll notice, about Jos watering the oleanders, though he is facing away from the Eglunds and Pastor Bruun.

—Being Danes, we had to have the Nielsen, and being lucky, we got to hear the Ives, but what sin were we being punished for with the Stravinsky? Ho, Mariana!

—It's sexist to piddle in public, she said, as you know I can't.

—Why not? Jos asked. Meg would, and has, if you count the woods and ferns. The showers. Scandalized Asgar.

—I'd ask you over, Holger said, except that Pascal and Alexandra are there.

—Horrifying, Jos said, zipping up. Isn't Pascal going to have to go to a rest home with an ice pack on his balls? Diet of thin gruel and wheatmeal biscuits? Babbling.

—Can't, anyway, Hugo said. We promised Franklin, who's sitting Barnabas, we'd be straight back. I gathered from some concupiscent observations he was making to Barnabas, who gurgled his approval, we can only suppose, that Alexandra had planned to be ravished by him this evening. But you say she's with Pascal.

—Worse and worse, Jos said, Hugo pretending to have forgotten the facts of life. I'm going to Holger's, infants fuckering in the middle of the floor or not. Mariana is going to kiss me goodnight.

—So's Hugo, said Hugo.

—Ork jo, Jos said. Style's all. When I have more style than anybody else in Denmark, the papers will ask me how I did it, and I'll say some from Mariana, some from Hugo, some from Holger, and NFS Grundtvig will be famous for something other than scouts who hold hands and thirteen-year-olds who are mistaken by the Geological Society for professors with beards down to here. Do we barge in, or is there a signal? We could go over the wall and give them a rude shock just as they're squishing in bliss. Barnabas has an orgasm from the top of his head to his pink toes when he's feeding at Mariana's teat, and so would I.

—Door's unlocked, Holger said.

—Ho! Jos called. Cultivated intellectuals back from the concert! Decent Lutherans wearing neckties!

—Alexandra's in the bathroom, Pascal said, getting dressed. Jos looks like the Stock Exchange.

—Why is Alexandra getting dressed? Jos asked. Why do I look like the Stock Exchange? Why are you kissing Holger and not me, too? Why don't you have on any clothes?

—Holger, hi, Alexandra said, tidying the sleeves of her sweatshirt. Hello, Jos.

—Hi, sprat. We, Holger and I, have been to hear the København Strygekvartet.

—They're lovely, Alexandra said.

—Hence these togs. At least one person, McTaggart the goofy English master, didn't recognize me. So what have you two been doing?

—Mind your manners, Jos, Holger said. I didn't recognize you when I first saw you this evening. Your eyes are shining, Pascal.

—Jos has manners, Alexandra said. I couldn't be the only person to see through Jos. He does everything a nice person can think of to be thought a big happy lout, whereas he's as gentle and well-bred a Grundtvigger as there is.

—And handsome, Jos said. Don't leave out handsome. So what were you doing?

—Well, Alexandra said, sitting and curling her naked toes, Pascal read me some of Holger's book, about fossil flowers and leaves, and some of an article of his about *une enfance différente, un peu effrayant mais pour la plupart sensible et bien pensé.*

—Style, Jos said. That's what I must work on. Style. Even Rutger has style. Nature's busy imperative stiffens his member when he sees Meg, but he talks a little politics and what's new in shirt collars before he shoves it in. Pascal and Holger snuggle in a sleeping sack in the wilds and talk about Finnish mosses and the poultry of Armenia.

—*Welwitschia mirabilis,* Pascal said, cogging his fingers among Alexandra's toes. Gnetophyta, country cousin with buck teeth of the conifers three hundred million years back. Genus with one species, as with angels.

—As with human beings, Holger said.

—They talk like this all the time, Alexandra sprite, and I'm going to talk like this, too, when I get the style down. As Pascal, who grew up with his nose in a book, turns into me, I need to turn into Pascal. I've worn the paper cutout wolfcub mask, crepitating on all fours, in red sneakers and whiffety blue pants, whining like a puppy, yapping silver yelps, and wagging my behind, sexy little tyke, and people were always taking my whiffety blue pants off, for one reason or another. This summer I sailed kites over at Malmö, in a park. All you wear's a pod of gauze strapped around the hips and up the crack of your butt. And bounced over the bay on a sailboard naked as I was born, curveting and skimming, hugging and tacking. And here I am, wanting to be Pascal, so's I can be an anthropologist and know all about people.

—I can't decide, Alexandra said, between anthropology and archaeology. I imagine I have a romantic view of both. I do, I'm afraid, of most things.

—Some more than others, Pascal said.

—What I want, Alexandra said, is a world where difference is not a way of being the same.

—Wait, Jos said, till I figure that out. I'm different, and stick out in the Grundtvig sameness. Why is Holger smiling?

—The really different person an outsider sees at Grundtvig is Mariana.

—O ja, Jos said. We all pant for Mariana, and slobber.

—Don't play the lout, Jos. Over at ES Brugge we're all being groomed for men like Hugo, even if they're too feminist to admit it, and Hugo goes for a woman who.

—Girl, Pascal said. Mariana's a girl.

—A woman who's decidedly lower class and of no family, as unsophisticated as she is ungrammatical.

—I hadn't noticed, Holger said. I mean, Mariana is Mariana. Hugo loves her. Clarissa Eglund consults her about hats, flowers, and sauces.

—Owl call, Jos said. Owl name of Franklin.

—Lend a back, Jos, Pascal said, to heave Alexandra over the wall.

87

Walt Whitman, sending some doughnuts to Horace Traubel's mother, wrote on the bag *not doughnuts but love*. It is, Holger said to Hugo, a useful formula. Of the yellow maple there in this autumn mist we might say *non acer est sed angelus*.

—It is, indeed, Hugo said. The opposite of a troll, wouldn't you say?

88

To *The British Grenadiers* on Pascal's fife and Sebastian's drum, followed by Kim with the guidon and Hugo with Barnabas on his back, the NFS Grundtvig Frispejderne, Tom White Gruppe, in two files of pairs holding hands, marched by Headmaster Eglund's house, out across the soccer field, and onto the country road.

—Aren't they, the headmaster asked Mariana, who was gathering roses with Clarissa Eglund, in different uniforms? I thought scouts were green and brown, not yellow and blue?

—And, Clarissa said, unless my eyes are deceiving me, little Barnabas has a uniform like the others. Did you see, Edward dear?

—I made it, Mariana said, exactly like the others, but with buttons on the blouse to anchor it to the pants. The pockets, of which there are six, gave me fits. Also made the flag. They're only going down the road a bit, for a practice patrol, and will be back in an hour or so, or Barnabas, who's the mascot, wouldn't be along.

—Sebastian, I believe, used to be a Tivoli drummer? What spirit to a drum and fife!

—Barnabas agrees, Mariana said. He does a kind of devil dance when Sebastian and Pascal practice. Hugo worked it out over the summer, I thought you knew. He made a scout troop of the revolutionaries. Denmark has about forty different kinds of scouts, Baptister Spejderkorps, Frivilligs, Communists, the Socialdemokratiske Ungdom, the fellowship this and the fellowship that, Greenland Pioneers, and whichwhat, so here's another. His own troop remains, the green and browns, with blue for the cubs, hr. Eglund was speaking of.

—Edward, please. So what are the mustards and slate blues?

—The Tom White group. They're like the Theban Band, it's called, in ancient Greece, pairs of friends. That's why they march holding hands, two by two. Jos keeps an eye on them, as an anthropologist he says, and Hugo has them all wanting to learn Greek and history, and Holger gave a wonderful talk to them on sharing time and space. A friend is another self, he said. Used words like respect and adoration and loyalty. Hugo said it was a sermon his father might have given. Barnabas, who was there with me, slept through lots of it.

—It's all well over my head, hr. Eglund said. Shall I do a bowl of roses, Clarissa dear? Anything to keep them out of mischief.

—Why, Clarissa asked, are they named for Tom White, and who was he?

—Somebody in the English army, I believe, Mariana said. Back when they wore red coats. Died terribly young. Hugo can tell you more about him.

—Yes, Edward, a bowl of roses for the table would be splendid.

89

—See? Pascal said, handing Holger a bunch of chicory and red valerian, they're flowers, for you, because Franklin brings them to Hugo, who puts them in a jar of water and says he likes them. They're sort of from the edge of fru Eglund's garden.

Holger laid a postcard in Kierkegaard's *Philosophiske Piecer*, to keep his place, and stared at the disarray of Pascal's hair, the livid welt on his cheek, his swollen lip that he played his tongue over.

—So will I put them in a vase, Holger said, if I have such an article. Which I absolutely don't.

—The marmalade, Pascal said, is down to just about enough to go on a slice of bread, with some butter, and then you'd have that to put the flowers in. Hugo keeps pencils in a marmalade jar.

A tear fattened in the corner of an eye and slid down his cheek, over the reddening welt.

—Ingenious solution, Holger said. And who do we know fossicking for tucker to finish off the marmalade with a cup of tea, perhaps?

—Milk, a big glass of cold milk. There's half a bottle and one not opened yet. You've been grading papers, all done, with the rollbook on top and a rubber band around the lot. And reading.

—Kierkegaard. Danish grasses and wildflowers, the papers. Now tell me what in the name of God has happened to you?

Pascal, eyes as round as kroner, was wiping marmalade out of the jar with his fingers.

—Franklin and I have had a fight. Alexandra's his girl only, now. I had it coming to me. Everything's OK, sort of. That is, we hit each other pretty hard. But he caught up with me afterward, when he cooled down a bit, to see if he'd hurt me. So we kissed and hugged, sort of.

His sandwich built of wedges of butter and runnels of marmalade, Pascal took as large a bite as he could, for the comedy of it, accepting a tumbler of milk from Holger.

—Pascal?

—All yours. Forever.

Typeset in Mergenthaler Sabon
by Wilsted & Taylor
with Clarendon display
Printed by Arcata Graphics/Fairfield
on acid-free paper